The Big Boys' Detective Agency

Stephen E. Stanley

The Big Boys' Detective Agency

Stonefield Publishing 2010

The Big Boys' Detective Agency

Author's Note:

Anyone familiar with Bath, Maine will realize that I have taken great liberties with the geography and history of the town. There is no All Souls Church. I have used the historic Winter Street Church as the setting, though it is no longer an active place of worship.

This book is a work of fiction. All characters, names, institutions, and situations depicted in the book are the product of my imagination and not based on any persons living or dead. Anyone who thinks he or she is depicted in the book is most likely delusional and should be institutionalized.

Stonefield Publishing
Portland, Maine
StonefieldPublishing@gmail.com

Author's Web page: http://stephenestanley.com/

 Special thanks to Louise Forseze for her support and copy reading skills and Raymond Brooks for his support in helping me free up time to write.

The Big Boys' Detective Agency

Stephen E. Stanley

Also by Stephen E. Stanley

A MIDCOAST MURDER
A Jesse Ashworth Mystery

MURDER IN THE CHOIR ROOM
A Jesse Ashworth Mystery

Cast of Characters

Jesse Ashworth—retired teacher and cookbook author with a newly minted detective license. After years working in New Hampshire, he has returned to his hometown of Bath, Maine.

Argus—a five year old pug dog from Kentucky. He is Jesse's best friend and constant companion.

Tim Mallory—former police chief of Bath, Tim is co-owner with his partner Jesse of the Bigg-Boyce Security Agency, nicknamed The Big Boys' Detective Agency by the locals.

Rhonda Shepard—retired New Hampshire teacher, she taught with Jesse for over thirty years, then moved to Bath and opened up a gift shop named Erebus. She loves vintage clothing and cake, not necessarily in that order.

Jackson Bennett—Jackson owns the largest insurance agency in Bath. He also is Rhonda Shepard's live-in boy friend.

Jason Goulet—Jesse's best friend. Jason, Tim, and Jesse went to high school together. Jason is married to Jesse's cousin Monica. Jason, at six foot seven, is a gentle giant.

Monica Ashworth-Twist Goulet—Monica married and went to Georgia to live until she divorced Jerry Twist. Like Jesse, she returned to Bath to begin a new life.

Billy Simpson—Billy and his ex-wife Becky were classmates of Jesse, Tim, and Jason. Billy finds mid-life to be challenging, but he is determined to find his place.

Jessica Mallory— Tim's daughter. She is a criminal justice major and works in Tim and Jesse's office.

Derek Cooper— a Bath police officer and part-time agent in the Big Boy's Agency. He is the man in Jessica's life.

Viola Vickner—a practitioner of the Wiccan faith, Viola works for Rhonda at Erebus.

Pastor Mary Bailey—the spiritual head of the liberal religious community, she is the pastor of All Souls' Church in Bath.

Kelley Kennedy—Jesse's ex-wife whom he hadn't seen for over twenty years. Jess is shocked when she turns up in an unexpected way.

John and Dorothy Lowell—Jesse's elderly neighbors on Sagamore Street. Dorothy was Jesse's second grade teacher,

Beatrice Lafond—An English teacher at Morse High for many years, Old Lady Lafond still takes an interest in her former students.

Clyde and Bonney Ashworth—Jesse's parents from Lakeland, Florida. It's best not to mess with this Bonney and Clyde.

William Baker—the Director of the Turner Art Museum in Portland.

Jacob Wright—homicide detective with the Portland Police.

John and Martha Rankin—the Rankins work and live at Beaver Lake, Maine, near the Canadian border. Martha is the cook at Beaver Lake Inn and John is the local handyman. John and Martha were college classmates of Brian Landry and Brian had been spotted in the area.

Connie Thurston—a Maine guide, Connie works in the northern woods.

Joyce Boyle—the curator of the Turner Art Museum in Portland.

Cindy Bishop—the summer cook aboard the windjammer *Doris Dean*.

Al Landry—Tim and Jesse's first client. The former police chief hires the agency to find his missing son.

Parker Reed— the skipper of the windjammer *Doris Dean* out of Camden Harbor. Currently dating Billy Simpson, he and Jesse have a history which Parker makes known he wouldn't mind renewing.

Bryan Landry—a security guard at the Turner Museum, Bryan walks off the job and disappears.

Chapter 1

The Big Boys' Detective Agency in Bath, Maine, is located on the upper floor of the Reynolds Block on Front Street. The actual name of the agency is *Bigg- Boyce Security and Investigations*, but everyone in town calls it the Big Boys' Agency.

I was staring at my newly minted private detective license, wondering how a retired school teacher ended up as a co-owner of a detective agency. I guess I was one of the Big Boys now!

The other owner is Tim Mallory, the former police chief. We share the business and a few other things as well, if you get my drift. When Tim retired from the police force we bought the agency. Actually, "bought" might be too strong a term. I think "took it off their hands" would be how Mr. Boyce and Mr. Bigg viewed it. Basically all we had to do was pay the back rent for the office, and for one thousand dollars we became the new owners of a less-than-thriving detective agency.

Money was not really an issue. Tim and I both had adequate pensions, so we were free to take cases or not, as we saw fit. The reception desk was run by Tim's daughter Jessica, who was doing her criminal justice internship with us, and we didn't have to pay her much. Right now the three of us were sitting around in the break room waiting for the coffee to finish brewing.

"Well, aren't we the balls!" said Tim.

"Hey, we just opened, don't panic! We're finally working for ourselves. Business should pick up soon," I assured him.

"I hope so, Stepdad," said Jessica. She called me Stepdad when she was being playful.

"Men of a certain age," I replied, "are too old to be called stepdad."

"Don't be bitchy," she replied with a wink.

"Language!" snapped Tim.

"Someone's cranky," observed Jessica. "And you said 'balls!'"

"Coffee is ready," I said and got up to pour three cups of the brew. We all needed the caffeine kick. I took my first sip as the phone rang.

"Bigg-Boyce Agency," answered Jessica. "Sure. Ten o'clock should be fine." She hung up the phone. "Client coming in at ten."

"Get ready!" Tim said to me.

"Sure," I said. "Let me clear my calendar."

"There's nothing on your calendar," he replied.

"There is now!" I answered and took another sip of coffee.

At 10:05 the door opened and a short, gray-haired man around the age of fifty, walked into the reception area. I was sitting at my desk playing with my mostly blank rolodex and listening as Jessica greeted him.

"Good morning! I called earlier. I'm Al Landry."

"Al!" I heard Tim's voice as I got up from my desk. "It's good to see you. It's been a long time." I was guessing that they knew each other. Great detective work on my part!

"This is my partner Jesse," said Tim as I walked into the room. "Jesse, this is Al Landry. He was the chief of police in Brunswick. He and I got promoted the same year and retired at the same time." We shook hands.

"Why don't we go into my office," suggested Tim. Tim's office is the bigger of the two and had a small conference table. Tim handled the face-to-face operation. My office, though smaller, is the tech center. I'm in charge of the high tech end of the business, and by high tech, I mean that I have a computer and a fax machine.

"Coffee?" I offered.

"Thanks, cream, no sugar."

"Tim?"

"Yes, please." I filled up the coffee cups and sat down.

"What can we do for you, Al?" Tim asked between sips of coffee.

"My son is missing. I was hoping you could help."

"You've filed a missing person's report?" I asked. As former cops Tim and Al just looked at me. It was a stupid question. "Of course you did," I added.

"They aren't much help. Adults can disappear and without evidence of foul play, there is very little they can do. No one has the manpower to launch an investigation," Al explained to me.

"But we do!" replied Tim. "You'll need to tell us a little more before we can agree to take the case."

Al Landry sat back in the chair and began his story.

When Al finished his account we had the basic facts. Bryan Landry, age twenty, was just out of college and working as a security guard at the Turner Art Museum in Portland. It was a small museum that featured Maine Artists and had a sterling reputation as one of the finest small museums in the northeast. The museum had been in the news about three days ago when a painting was stolen from one of the galleries. Bryan hadn't been working there at the time, so he was not a suspect.

Five days ago Bryan did not show up for work, yet his car was found in the gallery's parking lot. No word from Bryan since then.

"Has he ever done anything like this before?" asked Tim.

"Never! He is a very reliable kid," Al responded. "I'm sick with worry."

Tim got up, walked to door and asked Jessica to bring in a contract. He took the contract from Jessica, sat back down at the table, took a pen and crossed out the daily rate and wrote in a new one. "Professional discount," he said as he handed the contract over to Al.

"Thank you, Tim!" said Al with a sigh of relief.

"This case will be our first priority," answered Tim. Of course since we had just opened, it would be our *only* priority.

"It would be helpful," I said," if we could get into his place and look around."

"He has a small apartment in Portland on Westbrook Street. I have a key, too." Al scribbled down the address and passed me the key.

....

Early April in Maine looks much like early March. There are patches of packed snow on the ground and the air is cold. The only hint that spring might be on the way is the fact that the sun is higher in the sky than it had been during the short days of winter. If you looked closely at the trees, you could see the buds swelling up, but for the most part it is a dreary time of year.

I was walking up Sagamore Street with my dog Argus. Argus is a five year old pug who doesn't know he's a dog. At the end of the dead-end street sits a yellow bungalow with a sign on the porch that says "Eagle's Nest." The house belongs to me. I bought it several years ago when I retired from teaching in New Hampshire. Tim lives here with me now, having rented out his own house to his daughter. Jessica would be graduating from the university after she finished her internship. Currently Jessica is dating a local cop named Derek Cooper and she needs her privacy, so Tim had offered her his place.

I looked around the street as I walked toward the house. None of my neighbors were in sight. It is typical in New England that you can go for days in the winter without seeing your neighbors. Given the icy wind that was blowing, I think most people were wise to be inside.

I had left work early to walk Argus and make dinner. There wasn't a lot for me to do just now at the office. Tim was there and calling around to friends of Bryan Landry to see if they had any information or insight as to what might have happened to him.

Jessica was coming over for dinner and bringing Derek Cooper with her. I was planning on making meatloaf, oven roasted potatoes, and carrots. Nothing fancy, just hearty, good food.

I was in the kitchen when Tim pulled into the yard in his Subaru. Argus went off in a tear to greet him at the door. Tim came into the kitchen carrying a squirming Argus, opened the refrigerator and took out two beers. He put Argus down, twisted off the caps and passed one of the beers to me.

5

"Did you learn anything?" I asked taking the beer from him.

"Nothing useful. His supervisor at the museum says he was an excellent employee. His best friend insisted he wasn't depressed or in trouble."

"Girl friends?"

"None that any of his friends know about. I also used my police contacts in Portland. Officially, the case is open and ongoing."

"And unofficially?" I asked.

"Overworked, understaffed, bottom of the list."

"Maybe we'll learn something when we check out his apartment in the morning."

"Maybe," replied Tim, though not sounding very convincing as he said it.

Even in his uniform, Derek Cooper looked like a teenager. Dressed in a tee shirt and jeans, he looked even younger. Jessica and Derek sat at one end of the sofa and Tim sat in a chair opposite them. I was in the kitchen putting finishing touches on dinner. Derek always seemed to be ill-at-ease with Tim.

Derek was one of the last new hires that Tim made at the police department before he retired, and now Derek had just moved in with Tim's daughter in Tim's old house. Jessica, if she was aware of the awkwardness, didn't show it.

"We had our first case today," said Jessica to Derek.

"Really?" replied Derek. "That's cool."

"It's not too different from police work," began Tim. In a few minutes Tim and Derek were talking police talk and the tension had eased. I gave Jessica a high sign from the kitchen. She returned a wink.

6

"Dinner is ready," I said. Everyone piled into the kitchen.

"Smells great!" said Derek.

"Jesse is a great cook," Jessica told Derek. "He's even written two cookbooks!"

"Awesome," said Derek. "This tastes great!"

"Derek," began Tim. "I know how little beginning police officers make in Bath. I was wondering if you would like to freelance for us once in a while?"

"I'd love that!" answered Derek.

"You're the best, Dad!" replied Jessica.

The rest of the evening went smoothly. When Jessica and Derek went home I turned to Tim.

"I didn't know we needed a freelance agent?" I said.

"We don't, yet! But I think we will. It will also give me a chance to keep an eye on him. I don't want Jessica hurt. I know what police officers are like."

"Aren't they pretty much like you?"

"My point exactly!"

....

It was a gray morning with fog hanging over the town. It was misting slightly and the snow that was left was slowly melting in the forty degree temperature. The branches on the willow trees were showing signs of life and the buds were getting bigger by the day. The leaves of the daffodils were poking through the ground and there was every reason to believe that spring would arrive sometime soon.

Tim and I were having breakfast at Ruby's Restaurant on the waterfront before we drove to Portland to check out Bryan Landry's apartment. We were sitting at a small table by the window and had a great view of the river.

"Room for one more?" I looked up to see the six foot seven inch frame of Jason Goulet standing.

"Pull up a chair," I replied. Jason, Tim and I were high school classmates. Jason had also recently married my cousin Monica.

"How's business at the Big Boys' Agency?"

"We just got our first case," answered Tim.

"But, you've only been open for two days," observed Jason. Just then the waiter brought Tim and me our breakfast, and he took Jason's order.

"Tim was the police chief for twenty years," I replied. "He's built up a reputation."

"True enough!" agreed Jason. "Good thing you don't have to rely on Jesse's reputation. High school English teacher and cook book author just wouldn't inspire confidence. Unless of course you were tracking down a missing copy of *Hamlet* or a stolen recipe!"

"Goulet," I responded. "You have always been, and continue to be a total and complete asshole!"

"Back at you little guy!" he said to me with a smile.

"Hey," I defended myself, "I'm six-one!"

"Behave yourselves!" replied Tim. Jason's breakfast arrived and we continued catching up with the latest local news.

....

Bryan Landry's apartment was on the third floor of a large Victorian house in the Deering section of Portland. We let ourselves in with the key and walked up the three flights of winding stairs.

"I would hate to carry a refrigerator up these stairs," I remarked.

"Twenty-year olds don't worry about things like that," answered Tim.

The door opened into what was a fairly large studio apartment. There was a bed, a small sitting area with two easy chairs, a desk, a small kitchenette, and a separate bath.

"I'll search the room," said Tim. "You check out the computer."

I sat at the small desk and fired up Bryan's laptop. Tim was going through the closet and drawers looking for any clues. The hard drive was loaded with game programs and photo editing software. I checked them out, but I was more interested in his document folders and his email files.

"Find anything yet?" asked Tim.

"Nothing yet. I'm going to run a file recovery program just in case some important files have been deleted. Have you found anything?"

Not really. It's what I'm not finding. What does every young person have on them that they would never be without?"

"A cell phone?" I guessed.

"Exactly! When his father calls, it goes right to voicemail."

"So either he has it turned off or the batteries have run down!"

"Though it doesn't mean he has it with him."

"Bingo!" I said as I opened up the documents folder. "Bryan kept a list of all his passwords on a data base file. I'm going to print it out."

"Will that be helpful?" asked Tim.

"We'll see!" I answered.

9

Bryan had set his web browser to remember all his passwords. I was able to check his email and two of his accounts on social networking sites.

"I'm about done here," said Tim. "There are some empty hangers in the closet and a few missing toiletries. So he may have packed up a few things before he disappeared. Then again maybe they are just empty hangers."

"I'll take the laptop with me and work on it at the office. I'll give Al Landry a call and tell him I have Bryan's computer."

Tim and I straightened the place out, locked the door, and headed home.

Chapter 2

The first indication of spring came at sunset while I was taking Argus out for his nightly walk. Off in the distance I could hear the chirping of the spring peepers. The sound of those tree frogs was always the most welcome signal to the end of a long winter season. The damp, rather warm air smelled of earth and I knew that I could start digging in the garden.

My search of Bryan's computer had revealed some interesting findings. Several of the contacts in his email and social networking pages were from individuals located near Beaver Lake close to the New Brunswick border. Since this was a very remote and sparsely settled area of Maine, it was something that caught my eye. There were less than fifty full time residents of the township, and apparently Bryan was in touch with four of them. Other than that nothing else stuck out.

Bryan, like many young people, had his entire life on the computer. I went through his bank statement, his credit card accounts and his emails. Usually this was a difficult job, but Bryan had made it easy for me by bookmarking everything and storing his user names and passwords on his web browser.

Argus was nosing along the path enjoying the smells now that the ground was unfrozen. As we rounded the corner toward Eagle's Nest, my cell phone went off.

"How's business?" I recognized the voice of my cousin Monica Goulet.

"Actually, we have our first case," I answered. "An old business contact of Tim's hired us to find his missing son."

11

"I'm sure there will be a story there," she observed.

"I just hope we won't be wasting his money."

"I have a feeling you won't be," she said mysteriously.

"I'm sure you didn't call just to check on me. What's up?"

"I thought I'd give you a heads up."

"What about?" I asked.

"I was just chatting with your mother in Florida. She sort of hinted that she and your father might be coming up here to visit."

"What?" My parents had moved to Florida in 1989 and had never indicated any intention of coming back.

"It's just a heads up, but I thought I better prepare you before she calls."

"Thanks," I said. "I think." I hung up the phone. Maybe Monica was just playing with me. As it turns out, she wasn't.

....

Argus was curled up under my office desk. I took Argus to work with me every day. I was going through Bryan Landry's computer one more time, just to make sure I hadn't overlooked something.

"Any luck," asked Tim as he set a cup of coffee on my desk.

"Not really," I answered. "It's all pretty routine stuff. The only outstanding feature is that he has been in contact with four people in Beaver Lake."

"Where is Beaver Lake?" asked Tim

"It's in township thirty-two in Washington County near the Canadian border."

"What's the nature of the contacts?"

"Lots of inconsequential chit-chat, though some of it seems a bit cryptic."

"Can you print them out?" asked Tim.

"Way ahead of you, big guy," I said as I handed him the printed communications.

"Print out a map of the area and we'll go over these in my office. I'll ask Jessica to join us. She may be more familiar with computer talk than we are."

I fired up the mapping software, focused in on the Beaver Lake area and printed out maps of the area. Argus followed me into Tim's office and jumped into Jessica's lap. We passed the printouts around.

"Anything jump out to anyone?" asked Tim.

"Not really," observed Jessica. "Though the phrase 'big deal' seems to be repeated three times."

"I think we need to call the father and ask if these names mean anything to him."

"I can do that," offered Jessica.

"There are a series of emails from someone with the screen name Bugsy, but Bryan never responded to any of them."

"Any way to trace them?" asked Tim.

"No, they are from one of those free email web services. Almost anyone can create an anonymous email account," I responded.

. . . .

I hung up the phone and was staring off into space. Tim looked at me and noticed that I was still grasping the phone and seemed to be trying to crush it with my fingers.

"Something wrong?" asked Tim.

"That was my mother," I answered. "She just informed me that she and my father are flying into Portland next week and could I please pick them up?"

"I haven't seen them since high school," observed Tim.

"They moved to Florida in the 1980's and have never returned." I said. "Until now."

"We have a guest room."

"Thankfully they're staying at the Holiday Inn. They will be visiting with my aunts and uncles along the coast, but I have a feeling we will be expected to entertain them in the evenings."

"How bad could that be?" asked Tim.

"Don't even go there!" I warned.

Chapter 3

A gentle rain was falling as I took my cup of coffee out on the porch to watch the morning. I could hear Tim stirring around in the kitchen. Argus had elected to be in the kitchen with Tim, just in case a stray treat dropped to the floor.

"What's up today?" I asked Tim as he stepped out onto the porch. The three season back porch still had the glass windows, so it was nice and warm this morning. In a few weeks we would be able to remove the glass and put in the screens.

"I think we need to take a trip up to Beaver Lake and check out what Bryan Landry's connection is to the area."

"That's probably a six hour drive to Washington County," I said.

"We'll have to stay overnight. We'll need to keep expenses down. I don't want to run up Al Landry's bill too much."

"What about Argus?" I asked.

"I'll ask Jessica if she will take him. It shouldn't be a problem."

"Okay, where do we start?" I asked.

"We'll go to the office and take a look at the information we have, then we'll head up to Beaver Lake."

Thanks to the wonder of the computer age I was able to secure reservations at a lodge on Beaver Lake.

"And the most important thing is that the lodge has wireless internet access," I said. Jessica, Tim and I were sitting at the conference table going over the information we collected had so far.

"How about a view?" asked Tim.

"We have a Lakeside view. I think business is slow this time of year."

"Did you get any information from Al about the names we found on Bryan's computer?" Tim asked Jessica.

"Al didn't recognize any of the names, but he did say that he heard Bryan mention Beaver Lake one or two times. But I couldn't get any more information from him. He couldn't remember in what context Bryan had used the name. He said maybe it was a fishing trip."

"Well, that's all we have to go on at the moment." I said. "We'll check out the four people at Beaver Lake. We should be back in a few days.

"Don't worry, I'll take good care of Argus. And I'll hold down the fort here at the office."

"You're a good kid, Jessica!" I said.

"Shh! Don't ruin my reputation!" she answered.

....

The Big Boys' Detective Agency owned several nondescript cars for surveillance purposes. We chose an older Toyota Corolla to drive up to Beaver Lake. We took the highway as far as Bangor and then took route three across the state toward Washington County.

"Wouldn't it have been easier just to call these folks?" I asked.

"Sure and tip our hand. What if Bryan is hiding out with them and doesn't what to be found?"

"What is he hiding out from?" I asked.

"It could be anything. In any event we need to check out the Beaver Lake area before we start asking questions."

"So what are we going to do?"

"We are going to use our Boy Scout skills and spy on several of those cabins and see what's up?"

"We were never Boy Scouts," I reminded him. "We were only Cub Scouts. We never made the cut."

"Details, details. How much further is it to the lodge?"

"I'll check," I said as I punched in the address on the GPS. "According to this it's only an hour away."

"Jesus, we've been in this car for hours."

"And," I added, "it's only about twenty-five miles from here. I'm guessing that means that the road is rather primitive."

"Shit!" was all Tim said.

Beaver Lake Inn is a 1930s type log cabin lodge with a group of small log cabins located by the lake. It is some fifteen miles from the nearest town at the end of a dirt road. We checked in and were given one of the lakeside cabins. Meals were included and would be served in the main lodge. Breakfast and dinner were served in the dining room and box lunches were provided in the morning, so that the guests could spend the days boating or fishing or, in our case, spying.

"This is exactly what a lake cabin should look like," observed Tim as we stepped onto the screened front porch and then stepped inside. There was a king size bed, two big easy chairs, and a stone fireplace. There was a big closet and a small bath.

"What should we do first?" I asked.

"Let's unload the car and then how about a nap? It's been a long ride."

"Perfect!" I answered with a yawn.

We were cleaning up after our nap and unpacking when the dinner bell rang. The main dining room was huge with small tables set with white table cloths and kerosene lamps in the middle of each table. We found the table with our names on the place cards and were promptly waited on by a young waiter named Bob. We were presented with two choices for entrees: pot roast with vegetables or fresh haddock, broiled or fried. We both chose the pot roast and it was a good choice. Tender and juicy and served with mash potatoes and gravy, it had dandelion greens as a side dish.

"I haven't had dandelion greens since I was a kid," I said as I dug into my meal.

"Me either," agreed Tim. "It was always the first sign of spring when we could dig them up and have them for dinner. It was a treat."

"And a very short season," I added. "Once the dandelions blossom, they become too bitter to eat."

"And people spend hundreds of dollars a year to have them removed from their lawns!"

"So what's the plan?" I asked.

"I thought after dinner we would take a ride to get a general feel to the area and scope out where Bryan's friends live. It will be too dark to do much else."

Just then Bob came to our table and asked us if we would prefer pecan pie or molasses pie for dessert. It was a hard choice, but in the end we ordered molasses pie. Bob brought the pie and an order slip for tomorrow's lunch. The box lunches would be available to be picked up at breakfast.

The roads around the lake were no better than the bumpy dirt road we had to take to get to the lodge. We were able to locate the camps of Bryan's friends, but it was getting too dark to do any surveillance. We headed back to the cabin, pulled two beers out of the mini fridge and settled ourselves on the porch for the rest of the evening.

Chapter 4

The April breeze was damp and smelled of pine tree and earth as we made our way down a path by the lake. We had parked the car in a clearing beside the road that apparently served as a parking area for hunters in the fall.

We came to a small clearing on the path and had the first cabin in our sights. It was a small white clapboard covered cottage with Victorian accents. It belonged to two of Bryan Landry's cyber pals, John and Martha Rankin. We seated ourselves on a grassy slope to observe the house.

"What did you find for background on them?" asked Tim as he picked up a pair of binoculars.

"Actually quite a bit. They have their profiles on a social networking page. He is a local handyman who makes a living doing odd jobs around the area, and she is the head cook at the lodge."

"How did you find this out?" asked Tim.

"Jessica got the information. She sent a friend request to them and they answered. She's been chatting with them online. She sent me an email this morning. She tried to call you but couldn't get through."

Tim pulled out his cell phone and checked. "No signal!" he said as he put it away.

"I doubt if there are any cell towers around here," I replied.

"There's no cell phone coverage at the lodge but there is wireless internet?" asked Tim.

"Yes, go figure."

"Maybe the agency needs to buy a satellite phone."

"We'll be fine with just internet for the time being," I said.

Our conversation was interrupted by some movement at the house. We watched as a tall man left the house and headed to a late model pickup truck. The man got inside and started up the truck. We watched as the truck slowly wound down the dirt road and slipped out of sight behind the trees.

"What now?" I asked.

"We'll wait for a while and then go check out the cottage. If Martha is the cook at the lodge, she's probably there doing the cooking now." Tim reached into his backpack and handed me a rather large camera with a long lens. "Wear this around your neck."

"What are we taking pictures of?" I asked as Tim slipped a similar looking camera around his own neck.

"It's part of the disguise. If anyone sees us, they'll think we are bird watchers."

"There's one there!" I said as I spotted a brown bird in a nearby tree. "And there's another there! And there!"

"Very funny," answered Tim. "Now let's head down the path and check out the house."

As we got closer to the house it began to look a little more weather beaten than it had looked from a distance. We approached cautiously and scanned the area to make sure no one was watching us.

"Let's have a look," said Tim as he stepped up to a window. I moved around the house and peeked through another window. The cottage was basically one large kitchen and living area with one small bedroom and bath. There was nobody inside.

"No Bryan Landry hiding out here," I said.

21

"On to the next cottage," said Tim. "We still will want to talk to Martha when we get back to the lodge."

We returned to the car and drove halfway around the lake to the next cottage. It was owned by Ralph Walton, aged thirty, who worked in Portland as a manager of a small hotel. That was the only information Jessica could find on him. Jessica did have her boyfriend check police records, but none of the four friends of Bryan's had criminal records. I guess that was a good thing.

"This must be it," said Tim. The house was close to the road. We pulled up on the side of the road and got out. "I don't see any car tracks in the driveway. It doesn't look like it's been used in a while."

"Chances are," I replied, "that he only comes here a few times a year if he works in Portland. It's a long trip here even for a weekend retreat."

"Let's take a look anyway," suggested Tim. We left our cameras in the car this time. We were so far away from anywhere that it was unlikely that anyone was around to see us. Much like the first cabin there was no sign of Bryan Landry, or anyone else for that matter. This cabin hadn't been used for a while.

"Time for lunch," I said looking at my watch. It was a little past noon. I pulled two beers out of the ice chest in the trunk and we took the box lunches down by the lake and sat in two Adirondack chairs that Ralph Walden had conveniently set out under some trees.

"What now?" I asked when we had finished lunch.

"We should head back to the lodge and interview Martha Rankin. Then tomorrow we can finish by checking on the third cabin. Unless we find out anything new to help us find Bryan, we might as well head back to Bath."

....

The lodge kitchen was small, but amazingly efficient use of space made it seem ideal for cooking in a north country sporting lodge. Martha Rankin was peeling vegetables while Tim and I sat on stools at the prep table.

"Yes, he was here last week. He seemed upset, but he wouldn't say why. He stayed with us and seemed to relax. Two days ago we got up and he was gone."

"How did he get here?" I asked. "His car was left at the museum."

"He said he had driven up with a friend and that his friend had dropped him off here."

"Did he say who the friend was?" Tim asked.

"No, but I got the sense that it was a girl."

"How did you meet Bryan and become friends?" I asked

"We all met in college. John and I were a year ahead of Bryan. We came here right after college and started working. Bryan came up a few times during school breaks, but this was the first time he had come back here in months."

"Did he say anything about his job?" I asked.

"Just that he liked working for security at the Turner Museum, and would miss it."

"So you got a sense that he had quit his job?" Tim asked.

"That was the impression I got." Martha got up and washed the vegetables in the sink . She poured three cups of coffee from the large coffee urn and joined us at the prep table. "I don't mind telling you that I'm worried. I had no idea that his family reported him missing. And he left without even a good bye!"

"Does the name Bugsy mean anything to you?" I asked, referring to the unanswered emails on Bryan's laptop.

"No," replied Martha, though I thought I saw a hint of surprise in her eyes.

"How about Ralph Walton?" Tim asked. "He has a cabin on the other side of the lake."

"No, I don't know him, but I'm not from around here. John might know. He grew up here."

"The last name we have is Karen Carlson. She also has a cabin around here," I added.

"She's from around here and grew up with John."

"Do you think John would mind talking with us?" I asked.

"Not at all; he'll be as worried as I am when he finds all this out. Why don't you come around tonight after supper?" She wrote down the directions for us. We didn't bother to clue her in that we already knew our way to her cabin quite well!

. . . .

The morning was bright, but cloudy and a light rain was falling. It was just the perfect weather for turning the grass green after a long and bitter winter. It was not, however, the best weather for two detectives to venture out into the lakeside forest.

John Rankin had had little to add to our knowledge as to the whereabouts of Bryan Landry. He did give us some background on the fourth person,

Karen Carlson. It seemed she was a seasonal worker. She was presently in Florida working at a winter resort and would return to Beaver Lake to work at the lodge during its busy season. We could leave her off the list of people to interview for now, but we thought we should check out her cabin just to make sure Bryan wasn't holed up there.

The cabin, we learned, had been in her family for years. It was larger than most of the other cabins on the lake and was easily spotted from the water by the red color. Rather than drive over the rough roads, we borrowed a small boat with an outboard motor and headed across the lake.

"Do you know how to drive this thing?" I asked as I fastened my life vest securely around me.

"Not to worry," answered Tim as he pulled the starter cord on the rather ancient looking outboard. The motor caught and we headed across the water toward the red cabin.

"Hey Tim," I yelled pointing at the house as we got closer. "Look over there!" Near the boat dock we saw a figure in the distance walk to the edge of the woods and disappear. Tim turned the throttle up, the bow of the boat lifted out of the water and the boat shot across the water towards the house.

As we got near the shore, Tim turned the motor off and the boat landed gently on the small sand beach.

"Here, tie up the boat!" said Tim as he jumped off and went running off in the direction of the woods. I jumped out of the boat, tilted the motor out of the water and pulled the boat up on the beach. I took the rope and tied it to a tree, and followed after Tim into the woods.

When I stepped into the woods I could see neither Tim not the mystery person. I stopped and listened, but heard nothing. I watched too many *Twilight Zone* episodes when I was a kid, and I didn't like the fact that Tim had seemed to disappear into another dimension. I walked down the path stopping every few feet to listen for sounds, but all I heard was the chirping of some birds.

"Tim!" I yelled.

"Over here!" I heard Tim yell, but I couldn't tell from what direction. I heard the cracking of some branches and looked to my left and saw Tim emerge from the forest undergrowth.

"What's going on?" I asked. "Did you get a good look at him?"

"He ran into the woods, but I couldn't find him. He had quite a head start."

"Do you think it was Bryan?" I asked.

"No idea. But whoever it was didn't want to be found."

"It could be just a squatter taking up residence in an empty cabin."

"It could be but..." Tim began to speak and broke off as we heard a noise coming from the Lake.

"Shit!" Tim and I both recognized the sound of an outboard motor starting up. We both ran as fast as we could back toward the cabin. The boat was gone! Off in the distance we could see a figure in the boat as it slipped out of sight.

"Bastard!" said Tim. The figure was waving at us!

Chapter 5

I was sitting at my desk tallying up our expenses from our trip to Beaver Lake when Rhonda Shepard, dressed in a black 1940's lady's suit, complete with padded shoulders, waltzed into my office.

"What's new?" she asked as she plopped an oversized red purse on the edge of my desk.

"Since when do you carry a purse?" I asked. Rhonda and I taught at the same high school in New Hampshire for more years than either of us cared to admit. When she retired to my home town of Bath and opened a shop, I followed her here.

"Hey, it matches my shoes," she said as she lifted up her feet to show off her bright red shoes. "And answer my question. I haven't seen you in days!"

I told her about our adventure at Beaver Lake, until we got to the part about the stolen boat. She started to laugh so hard I thought she was going to pee her pants.

"And then what did you do?" she asked as soon as she could draw a breath.

"There wasn't much we could do. We checked out the cabin, but didn't find anything and then we began to walk back around the lake to the lodge. Fortunately John Rankin was out and about doing some errands and gave us a ride back to the lodge. When we got back the boat was tied up at the dock. But no one saw anything. It was a bit embarrassing, I have to admit."

"I can't wait to tell Jackson!" she said, referring to her live-in gentleman friend. He owns a local

27

insurance agency, and together they had just bought an ornate Queen Anne Victorian "cottage" on the river.

"Why don't you both come to dinner tonight and we can all get caught up?" I suggested. Just then Tim stepped into my office.

"Hello, Rhonda," he said and then turned to me. "We have an appointment in about forty-five minutes and a possible new case."

"Well, then if you will excuse me," said Rhonda getting up out of the chair. "I'll see you both tonight." We watched her leave the office.

"She's too much," observed Tim.

"You don't know the half of it," I said. "So what's the new case?"

"Wait and see, 'cause you won't believe me if I tell you!"

....

The man sitting across the conference table looked ordinary enough. Middle age, slightly balding, big glasses, he looked like a manager of an accounting firm. Instead he was the executive director of the Turner Art Museum in Portland.

"You want us to find a ghost?" I asked incredulously.

"Of course not!" replied William Baker patiently. "I guess I need to explain. I want you to prove that the gallery is not haunted. Our staff is coming in to work some mornings and noticing that things have been moved around and changed. I want you to find out who or what is causing this."

"Why aren't you using your own security staff?" I asked.

"I want absolute discretion, and well," he said, "my security officers are top notch, but I don't trust them to be discrete. Besides, one of them might be involved. I need to outsource this job."

"I see," said Tim. "I think I understand."

"Here is a small retainer if you should decide to take the case." Mr. Baker reached into his jacket pocket and pulled out a check and pushed to towards me. One look at the check and I nodded to Tim.

"We would be happy to take the case," said Tim. He gave Mr. Baker a list of our prices and a contract. William Baker signed the contract, and we all shook hands. We walked him to the door and told him we would start tomorrow.

"Run to the bank and cash this," I said to Jessica as I tossed the check on her desk. "If it doesn't bounce, we're in business!" Jessica picked up the check, looked at the amount and gave a low whistle.

....

"So what, exactly, are you working on for a case?" asked Jackson Bennett. Jackson was leaning against the kitchen door as I was putting a pan of spaghetti pie in the oven.

"Well, we have a missing person's case and we are working security for a non-profit organization. That's about as detailed as I can be, client confidentiality and all," I replied as I set the oven timer.

Jackson and I returned to the living room where Rhonda and Tim were deep in conversation. Tim stopped long enough to fill our wine glasses.

"So what's on the menu?" asked Rhonda as I sat down beside her on the sofa.

29

"I'm afraid it's nothing fancy. Now that I'm working again, I have to find easy to prepare comfort food. It's spaghetti pie and salad."

"What the hell is spaghetti pie?" asked Tim. I could tell he was envisioning a pastry shell filled with pasta.

"It's a layered meat and cheese dish like lasagna, only it uses spaghetti instead of noodles. It's much quicker to prepare."

"And dessert?" asked Rhonda. "There better be cake!" Rhonda has two passions; vintage fashion and cake.

"Applesauce cake," I answered.

"I was just telling Rhonda," said Tim, changing the subject, "that we hired Derek Cooper to work part time for us."

"He and Jessica make such a sweet couple," observed Rhonda. Tim rolled his eyes.

"I agree," I answered, "but Tim doesn't think anyone is good enough for his daughter."

"Typical," replied Jackson, who had two adult children of his own.

"So," I asked Jackson, "how is the new house working out?" Rhonda and Jackson had recently bought an old historic Queen Ann Victorian by the river. Moving in together was a compromise as neither seemed interested in marriage.

"It's very drafty on windy days, but when the weather is sunny and warm, it's a great place," he answered.

"I'm sure it was built as a summer retreat, and they weren't so concerned about the winter," added Rhonda.

Just then the kitchen timer went off. I went into the kitchen and took the spaghetti pie out of the oven to cool, sliced up some bread, and put the salad out. Tim set the table and refreshed everyone's drinks. I plated the food and served everyone and then sat down.

"This tastes great," said Tim.

"You are the king of comfort food," agreed Rhonda.

"It always tastes better when someone else does the cooking," I replied.

"So when are your parents coming?" asked Rhonda. "I can't wait to meet them."

"Meeting them will be an experience," Tim chimed in.

"They are arriving tonight and checking into the hotel. They said they would be here for breakfast in the morning," I said as Tim rolled his eyes."

....

My father was recovering from hip surgery and sat on the edge of the easy chair in my living room leaning on his cane. My mother was recovering from a bad hair day.

"Your hair burner should be shot!" I said to my mother, who was bustling around in my kitchen, insisting on cooking breakfast for everyone.

"I've used Gina Cooper for years. She always did my hair before we moved."

"Gina Cooper is one step away from the dementia ward," I replied. My mother's hair was tinted bright red and cut in a style that was in fashion back in 1953.

31

"You really should get some new Teflon cookware," said my mother. I watched Tim roll his eyes as he watched my parents. He was waiting for breakfast and I knew he would be out the door and to the office as fast as he could.

"So what exactly was it that made you two think you could run a detective agency?" My father directed the question to Tim.

"If you remember, I was chief of police here in town, and your son is extremely intelligent."

"Yes, he is," my father conceded. "But he's never had a real job." My father didn't consider teaching to be a real job.

"Dad…" I began, but my mother shot me a warning look. Fortunately the door bell rang and Monica stepped into the house.

"Just in time for breakfast," said my mother as Monica hugged both of my parents.

"Monica has offered to drive us to Belfast to visit my sister," informed my mother.

"I have some Valium in the bathroom, if you need it," I whispered to Monica.

"Thanks, I'll take the bottle with me," she replied with a wink.

"Breakfast is ready!" informed my mother. We all went into the kitchen and sat down as my mother filled our plates with food.

"How long are they staying?" asked Tim as we left the house and headed to the car.

"Two very, very long weeks."

"You certainly didn't learn to cook from your mother, did you?"

"No, I learned to cook in self defense." I replied. My mother had served us hard, rubbery eggs, fatty bacon, and burned toast. She blamed it on my cast iron cookware.

"Maybe I should go back to Beaver Lake and check on things," suggested Tim.

"Oh, no! You are going to suffer with me," I said.

"Bastard!" answered Tim as we drove off to work.

When we arrived at the office I checked the message on the answering machine. There was one message and it was from John Rankin in Beaver Lake. I dialed the number.

"Hi John, it's Jesse Ashworth. What's up?"

"Mary thinks she saw Bryan Landry."

"Tell me about it," I suggested.

"Well, Mary was driving back home from the lodge. She saw Bryan walking along the road. She went past him and stopped the car. When she got out Bryan had disappeared."

"And she's sure it was Bryan?" I asked.

"Oh, yes. And she's sure that he saw her as well."

"Okay, thanks John. I'll be in touch," I said and hung up. This was getting interesting.

33

Chapter 6

It was late afternoon and it was still light outside. We had set the clocks ahead in the annual Daylight Saving Time mode, and the daylight did seem longer. We arrived at the Turner Museum about one hour before closing. William Baker ushered us into his private office.

"I'd like you to pose as security guards for the next week. That would give you the opportunity to look around without drawing suspicion. It will also give you a chance to check out the other guards."

"Actually there are three of us. I'd like my part time investigator to be part of this too," said Tim, referring to Derek Cooper."

"Even better!" said Baker.

"Derek has the day off tomorrow, so I'd like him to start first. We'll come on board in the next couple of days. That way it won't look like we all arrived at once," suggested Tim.

"Perfect" said Baker and we left for home.

"I'm having a hard time multitasking," I said to Tim when we got back to the office. "Working on two cases at once is confusing."

"Well, that's nothing compared to ordinary police work. Think of them like classes. You've taught different classes and subjects at the same time."

"That's true enough," I agreed.

"And we really can't do anything about the museum case until we actually start, so let's work on Bryan Landry's disappearance."

"Okay, so where are we in that case?" I asked.

"Bryan disappeared. He didn't show up for work, he hasn't contacted his father. Both events are uncharacteristic behaviors for him, we are told."

"We also know that as of last week he was alive and visiting friends in Beaver Lake," I added. "And he disappeared from their house, but they may or may not have seen him recently."

"The missing key here," said Tim, "is that we have no idea why he disappeared. Maybe if we knew that, we could figure out what the hell is going on."

"At least we were able to tell his father that he is alive," I observed.

"True enough. That was a big relief for the father."

....

Derek Cooper was sitting in my office in full uniform. He had just finished his first shift at the museum and was about to begin his shift at the police department. Jessica was standing in back of him and rubbing his shoulders.

"How was your first day?" I asked.

"It was pretty good. I was able to meet some of the younger guards and get the gossip about the place."

"What did you tell them about yourself?" I asked.

"I was honest, so I wouldn't get caught in a lie. I said I was a rooky police officer and I was working at the museum because I needed some extra cash."

"Good thinking," I said.

"And how many of these young guards," asked Jessica, "are women?" I noticed Jessica's massage of Derek's shoulder got just a bit more aggressive.

"Only one," answered Derek. "And she weighs three hundred pounds." Derek shot me a wink that Jessica couldn't see.

"And what were your impressions of the place?" I asked.

"Everyone there is friendly, but there is something there that I just can't put my finger on."

"I'm sure we can unravel it all in time," I replied.

"Well, I need to go off to my real job," said Derek as he got up to leave.

"I'll leave you two alone to say good bye." I got up and went into the break room. Argus, who had been sitting under my desk all morning, got up and followed me.

The break room had a kitchen from the time when the upper floors of the Reynolds Block contained apartments.

Since I had started working again fulltime, I hadn't been able to do as much cooking. Slowly I had stocked the office kitchen with basic resources. Cooking always gave me time to sort out my thoughts, as well as coming up with healthy, non-processed food. I decided to make a batch of blueberry muffins for the morning break.

Just as I put the muffins in the oven a thought occurred to me about the Landry case. Food! Somehow Bryan Landry had to feed himself. That meant he either was going to restaurants, or he was buying groceries somewhere. It would be worth it to visit some grocery stores and restaurants with a picture of Bryan. Maybe someone, somewhere had seen him. It was worth a try.

"I think one of us needs to go back to Beaver Lake," I said to Tim as I placed two warm blueberry muffins on his desk. I went on to explain my thoughts on the matter.

"It's worth a try," Tim said as he picked up a muffin and devoured it in one gulp. "You want to do it?" he asked me. Argus jumped into Tim's lap and proceeded to look for crumbs.

"Sure," I replied. "It really only needs one person to go there. I can probably cover the area in one day."

"Great! But not until your parents go back to Florida. You are not leaving them with me!"

"Shit! I forgot about them."

"I'll bet you did!"

....

It was Sunday morning and Tim, Derek and I were scheduled to be the security team at the Turner Musem. It was our job to open up the museum, shut off the security alarm, do a walk-through of the gallery, and open the safe to replenish the cash supply for the admissions desk. After opening, we would be stationed in different areas of the museum to make sure the visitors behaved themselves.

"Derek," said Tim, who was designated as the lead guard of the day, "would you go outside and do a perimeter check of the building?"

"Yes, sir," answered Derek as he headed out the door.

Tim turned to me, "I'll go to the safe and you can do an interior check of the galleries."

I was halfway through the galleries when I heard the crackle of the walkie-talkie. It was Derek.

"Assistance needed at the rear of the museum at the loading dock."

37

"Copy that!" said Tim from somewhere in the building.

"Copy," I said as I headed to the loading dock.

At first I didn't see anything amiss when I arrived at the loading dock. I expected to see a delivery truck with food for the museum's café. Tim arrived and then we both saw Derek leaning over what looked like a bundle of rags.

"Call the police," said Derek. "It looks like she's dead." Tim and I stepped closer and saw a woman lying in a pool of blood. I was going to ask if she was breathing, but Derek anticipated the question and just shook his head.

"Don't touch anything," said Tim unnecessarily. "Take a closer look at what she's wearing."

I stepped closer to look at the body. It was a middle-aged woman lying face down, and she was dressed in what looked like a majorette uniform.

"Not really age appropriate," I observed and then stopped short. "There's something familiar about her."

"What is it?" asked Tim.

"I don't know exactly. But I think I've seen her someplace before."

Chapter 7

The sun was warm as the morning progressed. It had been a cold spring with periods of warm weather several days at a time. Today promised to be one of the warmer days. People were gathering at the entrance of the museum, only to see a hand-lettered sign informing them that the museum was temporarily closed. Even though the loading dock was in the back of the museum and out of sight, a crowd was gathering behind the crime tape that cordoned off the area.

The police were busy taking measurements and photos of the crime scene. Tim, Derek and I were in the security office watching the police activity on the security cameras. Police detective Jacob Wright was taking down our statements.

"You said, Dr. Ashworth, that the deceased looks familiar to you?"

"No, I said that there was something about her that looked familiar. She was face down so I couldn't see her face. It's just that something about her is bothering me," I answered.

"Well, we should get an ID on her soon. Once we get the evidence from the area we can go through her purse and check for identification."

"There is something you should know," began Tim, "off the record." Tim went on to tell Detective Wright why we were working there.

The medical examiner and his staff had arrived and they were preparing to remove the body. Detective Wright left to join the others. William Baker, the museum director had arrived on the scene looking extremely upset and was being brought up to date on the events by the police team on the scene. We watched

39

Detective Wright gesture in our direction and we knew Baker would be joining us soon.

"This is a nightmare!" exclaimed Bill Baker as he entered the room followed by Detective Wright. "There's something I've got to show you." Bill Baker exited the room. We all looked at each other puzzled.

"Take a look at this!" Bill Baker had a photograph in his hand and he passed it to Wright. We moved around and looked over his shoulder.

"Holy shit!" said Tim. The photograph Bill Baker was holding was of a painting. The subject of the painting was an older woman dressed up as a majorette.

"It's the same uniform!" I observed unnecessarily.

"This," said Baker with tears in his eyes and shaking the photo at us, "is the painting that was stolen from the museum!"

Before any of us could react, another detective entered the room and passed a note to Detective Wright.

"We have a tentative ID on the victim," he announced. "Her name is Kelley Kennedy."

The room seemed to grow dim and gravity seemed to have deserted me as I lowered myself to a chair.

"Something the matter?" asked Detective Wright.

I opened my month to speak, but nothing came out. "Relax and breathe," said Tim as he placed his hands on my shoulders and began to rub them.

"What's going on?" asked Wright.

"Kelley Kennedy is Jesse's ex-wife!" replied Tim.

. . . .

It was close to eighty degrees and no breeze anywhere. It was the warmest day of the spring so far and everyone was outside enjoying the weather. I was surprised at how fast people had shed their winter clothes and donned shorts and flip-flops. The police station was stuffy, but at least I was in an office and not in an interrogation room.

"When was the last time you saw Kelley Kennedy?" asked detective Wright.

"I haven't seen her in twenty-five years. We were divorced and went our separate ways. I didn't even know she was in Maine."

"You just took an assignment at the Turner Museum. She worked in the office as a grant writer. You didn't know she was here?"

"No, I didn't. I've only worked security twice and both times the offices were closed."

"And what was your relationship with her like?"

"As I said," I was growing tired of this. "I hadn't seen or heard from her in twenty-five or twenty-six years. We left on good terms; but that was all so long ago."

"And yet," continued Detective Wright, "you recognized the body after twenty-five years."

"I did not," I insisted, "recognize her. I said there was something familiar about her."

"So you did," agreed Wright. "And where were you last night around nine o'clock?"

"I was at home in Bath."

"And did anyone see you there?"

"Of course! Tim Mallory was with me." I said. "All night!" I added just to make it clear.

"Okay, Dr. Ashworth. Thanks for answering our questions. You're free to go." I expected him to tell me not to leave town, but he didn't.

Tim was waiting for me. He had been with another detective answering questions.

"Am I a suspect?" I asked Tim.

"No. You have an alibi and no known motive. But they have to rule you out. They told me she was most likely killed between nine and ten last night and you were far away."

....

"Why was she dressed up as a majorette?" asked my mother. Both parents were sitting in my living room looking at me for answers.

"I have no idea; we've been divorced for years."

"She was a strange one," added my father. "I always wondered what you were thinking." That's the great thing about parents. No matter how much you've grown up, to them you will always be the awkward, clueless teenager who needs constant reminders about how clueless you are.

"I've always said she was going to end up badly," said my mother. My mother had never said any such thing. Maybe her hair dye was toxic and that was affecting her memory.

My parents were due to fly back to Florida tomorrow. I knew Tim would be relieved to see them go. As for me, I couldn't wait for them to hit the friendly skies!

"We could always stay an extra week if you need us," offered my father. I saw the panic in Tim's eyes.

"Thanks," I said. "But I have Tim and Monica to take care of me." I didn't add that at my age I was completely able to take care of myself.

"Let's go out for dinner tonight," said Tim to change the subject before my parents could change their minds about leaving. It was a perfect plan. We could drop them off at their hotel after dinner and have some alone time.

"Sure thing," said my father. "But it's my treat. No sense arguing."

I didn't point out that no one was going to argue about the bill.

"Let's pick up Monica and Jason on the way," suggested my mother. "She's family."

"So are Tim and Jason," I said.

"Oh, of course," she replied, but I think she knew I caught her in one of her word games.

"I'll give them a call," said Tim as he picked up the phone and suppressed a grin.

Monica and I were up early and drove my parents to the airport in Portland. It was a clear day, and I was sure their flight would be a smooth one. Florida was just over a three hour flight so they would be home in plenty of time for their afternoon naps.

"Thanks for helping out with them," I said to Monica as we waved back at them as they stepped through security.

"They are my aunt and uncle after all, and family is family," she said as she rolled her eyes.

"Yes, they are, aren't they?" I replied.

"Let's go shopping!"

"Okay," I agreed. "Let's go to the old port."

It only took a few minutes to drive from the airport to the old port section of the Portland. It took another ten minutes to find a parking spot in town. I finally gave up and parked in a parking garage. We walked down the street towards the waterfront and found a coffee house, ordered coffee, and sat at a table near the window.

"So, how are you doing?" asked Monica. "It must have been quite a shock."

"That's the strange thing. We were married for five years. I ought to feel something, but it was so long ago it seems like something I saw in a movie once. I have visual images, but not any real memories."

"I think it's different when you have kids. I'll always be attached to Jerry Twist because of my two boys, even though Jerry is a complete asshole. You had no kids and no communications for twenty-six years. Whoever she had become, it had nothing to do with you."

I looked around the coffee house and out toward the street. Everything seemed normal to me. "My sixth sense seems to have left me," I said. Monica and I had been brought up in a family that embraced Spiritualism. Talking to the dead and having active intuitions had been a regular part of our lives. Neither of us really believed in it anymore; but from time to time we had feelings and experiences we couldn't ignore.

"I know what you mean," replied Monica. "I think when the dust settles after a few days, we might get some insight. Do you know what I think?"

"Not really."

"I think that the sixth sense is really the subconscious taking bits of information and putting it together, and then giving our conscious mind a swift kick start. Most people have been taught to ignore it. We were taught to pay attention and listen."

"That makes perfect sense," I said, somewhat relieved. "Maybe in a day or two, when we get more information, the sixth sense will kick in again."

"Or maybe your spirit guides are just taking a break," said Monica with a laugh.

"Finish your coffee," I said. "We've got shopping to do!"

Chapter 8

After the spring rains the sun had returned, and everything began to break into bloom. According to my journal, everything was about a week and a half early. I wasn't complaining. I was sitting on the back steps warming myself in the sun and watching Tim mow the lawn. Tim was shirtless and sweating and I was watching his shiny, muscled torso gleam in the sun. Since Tim had moved in, we had split up the chores. I did the gardening and cooking. Tim did the mowing and housework. It was a great arrangement, and the fringe benefits weren't bad either.

Argus was sitting beside me watching Tim work, when he suddenly bolted upright and ran for the back door. I went into the house to find Rhonda at the front door.

"Come on in," I said. "Coffee?"

"You bet," she replied. Argus was so excited to see her that he ran around her in circles.

"He hasn't had any company for days," I explained. "Let's go sit on the back porch and have our coffee. I also whipped up some strawberry muffins"

We went out to the back porch. Tim had taken down the glass panels and put in the screens for the summer. The back porch was my favorite room in the house.

"Nice view," remarked Rhonda as she watched Tim mow. "He looks like an underwear model."

"I'm pretty sure he's not wearing underwear." Tim saw us on the porch and waved. We waved back.

"He has no clue, does he?" remarked Rhonda.

"None at all. He thinks he looks like everyone else."

"I came to see how you were doing. After all you found your ex-wife dead."

"Actually Derek found her and at the time I didn't know who she was. It's all very strange. It has brought back some good memories and some bad ones. But the strange thing is I don't really feel much of anything."

"You don't have to explain to me. I've been married four times and I don't even remember anything about number one."

"How are things at the store?" I asked to change the subject. Rhonda owned a gift shop named Erebus on Front Street. I had worked for her part time handling Internet sales until Tim and I bought the agency.

"Viola has managed to take over the Internet sales and is doing quite well. I was able to add her on full time."

"And you've managed not to kill each other?" Viola Vickner is an interesting person. She is a witch, who is a practicing Pagan and she dresses the part. Her eccentric style often clashes with Rhonda's vintage fashions. Some days it's a full out fashion war.

"I've warned her not to wear denim jumpers and so far she hasn't." Rhonda hates all things denim on women. On men she loves it. I've pointed out the sexism of this, but all I got was a rude gesture.

"And business is going well?" I asked.

"Better than I ever thought."

"And do you miss teaching?"

"Sometimes, but not very often. It all seems so long ago."

"I miss working with the kids, but not living by the bell."

"What's going on?" asked Tim. He had put on a shirt, grabbed a cup of coffee and joined us on the porch.

"Just admiring the view," said Rhonda.

"It is a beautiful backyard," agreed Tim. Rhonda and I just looked at each other and laughed.

"What's so funny?" he asked.

"Inside joke," I said. The phone rang and Tim got up to answer it. He talked briefly and then hung up. He returned to the porch and sat down.

"That was the Portland police. Kelley Kennedy's next of kin has been notified. The autopsy is scheduled for Monday, and no final arrangements have been made yet."

"Kelley had a sister and brother in New Jersey," I said. "But that's the only family I know of."

"There is a husband," said Tim.

"Is he a suspect?" I asked.

"The investigators are checking his alibi. But the police always suspect the spouse first."

"Did you know she had remarried?" Rhonda asked me.

"I had heard that she had, but don't know anything about it."

"I should get to the shop before Viola gives the place away," said Rhonda getting up.

"What do we do now?" I asked Tim.

"Derek and I will continue at the museum. I think now would be a good time for you to go to Beaver Lake."

....

I drove up route one through the small coastal towns, enjoying the warm air and the smell of the sea. I had the sun roof open for the first time since last fall. My thoughts kept returning to Kelley. We had met in college and had been happy, but real life wasn't like college. Career pressures and immaturity had taken their toll and we divorced, as had most of my friends back in the eighties. In fact a group of us teachers at Amoskeag High had started our own informal divorce club.

I stopped in Waldoboro for lunch at Moody's Diner. It was the first restaurant I ever visited as a kid. It was one of the few things in my life that had not changed. It looked much the same as it had back then. I ordered the turkey dinner and finished it off with a piece of homemade blueberry pie.

Back in the car I traveled through Camden and Belfast and up to Bangor where I stopped for a cup of coffee. The longest part of the trip would be from Bangor to Beaver Lake, much of it over winding route nine. I put on some classical music and enjoyed the ride. I arrived at the Beaver Lake Inn during the late afternoon.

After checking in and unloading my stuff, I made my way to the kitchen where Martha Rankin was taking pies out of the oven.

"Hi, Jesse," she greeted me. "I wasn't sure when you were coming."

"I just arrived and thought I'd check in with you first."

"I hope you don't mind if I keep working. My assistant called in sick today." Martha picked up a potato and started to peel it.

49

"Let me help." I grabbed a peeler and started to peel.

"Thanks, Jesse. I hate peeling potatoes. Well, let me start at the beginning. I was driving to work. It was a foggy morning and the main road had been flooded out by the recent rain. I had to take the old logging road, which takes me about five miles out of the way, but it usually doesn't get affected by the rain. Anyway as I rounded the corner I almost ran into Bryan. He looked surprised to see me. He jumped out of the way and I slammed on the brakes and jumped out of the car. When I got out he was gone."

"And you think he recognized you?" I asked.

"Oh, yes. Our eyes locked for a second. He saw me alright. Besides, he knows the car."

"And he just disappeared?" I was on my fifth potato and tired of peeling.

"Yes, but I could hear him crashing around in the undergrowth. I tried to follow, but I couldn't."

"So is there anything out there on the old logging road?" I started peeling carrots while Martha cut up the potatoes.

"There's an old logging camp out there and an old locomotive steam engine that's rusting on a set of old railroad tracks. There are a few small hunting cabins in some of the remote areas. Most of the logging roads are grown up and you can't get a car through there."

"Bryan could be anywhere then. Most likely camping out," I said.

"Yes, but I don't understand why he would be hiding."

"And that," I said, "is the key to the whole mystery.

After a very nice dinner, I retired to my cabin and turned in early, vowing to be up early and to explore the area around the logging road. After a hearty breakfast I picked up my box lunch, packed my backpack and walking stick, and struck out to the old logging camp.

I went as far as I could with the car, and then parked it off the side of the road. I left a note in the car, outlining my hiking plan as a safety measure and headed up the dirt road. I took out my GPS and placed a waypoint at the parking lot so that I could find my way back again.

The road became more and more obscure and overgrown as I headed toward the old lumber camp. I wasn't sure exactly what I was looking for. Would it be a fallen down set of buildings or just an old cellar hole? It seemed as though I had hiked forever and I sat down to rest. My GPS informed me that I had only hiked about a mile. I sat under a tree and ate an orange and had some water. I reapplied mosquito repellant and headed up the road.

In about half a mile, a set of old, rusty railroad tracks crossed the logging road. I turned right to look down the rail path and saw the rusting hulk of the old steam engine. I took a detour and headed down the tracks to check it out. The engine was massive and even though it was rusted and abandoned, it still gave the impression of power and strength. I could just imagine it in its heyday, loaded with flatbeds of logs heading to the paper mills at Rumford and Westbrook.

I returned to the logging road and in a few minutes I came into the logging camp. There were several gray weathered buildings with metal roofing. Some of the buildings were in near collapse and others were in better shape. There were machines and saws

51

blades of various sizes, all rusting in a fallen-down shed. The logging operation had ceased sometime in the 1970's. The entire place had a spooky feeling to it. It looked like one day everyone had just walked away.

I didn't see any evidence that anyone had been here for a while. Most hikers are considerate and carry out what they carry in. I was about ready to head back when I spotted a bit of blue off in the distance.

As I got closer I could see that the blue was a piece of a small tent. The tent was fairly new. I looked under the tent floor and saw that the grass was still green, so it hadn't been up long enough to kill the grass. I unzipped the front, there were no sleeping bags or cooking instruments. I jotted down the brand and model of the tent in my little notebook. I found a pile of empty dehydrated food containers in a small pile of garbage not far from the tent. Whoever did this was not an experienced camper. Keeping food containers outside near the campsite was a great way to invite animals to your camp site.

I jotted down the information on the food containers, took photographs, sketched out the camp site in my notebook and headed back to the car.

The walk back seemed easier and the GPS was able to give me an update on my progress. As it happened, the walk was just over two miles back to the car. On the way I was able to look around and appreciate the beauty of the late spring forest. Just as I rounded a corner I came face to face with three deer. I stopped dead in my tracks. They stopped and we stared at each other for a few seconds. Slowly the deer moved and then ran off in the woods with their tails wagging. It was a magical moment.

52

The magical feelings disappeared, however, when I got back to the parking lot. Someone had smashed out the front windows of my car!

Chapter 9

The day was heating up and the scent of pine was in the air. Off in the distance I could hear the birds singing and the blue sky was filled with puffy white clouds. It was a perfect day, except for the fact that my car window was smashed out and most of it was decorating the interior of my front seat.

I flipped open my cell phone, but as I expected there was no service in this remote area. I sat on a rock under a tree and took out my lunch. No use worrying on an empty stomach. The inn had packed me a nice lunch of ham salad sandwiches, carrot sticks with dipping sauce, an apple, and a chocolate cup cake. I had a bottle of water, but a nice cold beer would have been better.

After my lunch I went into the trunk and took out a blanket. I rolled it up and used it to sweep out the front seat and get as much of the glass out as possible. I started to drive back to the inn. I had to drive slowly because the wind coming in through the window was, to say the least, distracting. I never realized how many insects there were out there until they all started to hit me in the face.

Once back at the inn I called the nearest auto glass shop. They said they would send out a repair truck tomorrow. The insurance company didn't sound happy when I called, but too bad for them. Since I wasn't able to do any more investigating today, I would have to stay an additional day.

I took out my phone card and gave Tim a call.

"What's up?" asked Tim when I called the office. I told him about going to the logging camp and about what I found.

"Good work!" he replied.

"There's more." And then I told him about the smashed out window.

"At least you have some leads to follow."

"How's everything there?"

"We're fine. Argus misses you and so do I."

"Me, too!" I replied. "Anything new about the murder?"

"The autopsy indicated a severe head trauma. No weapon or motive or suspects at this point. Since the area around the body was clean, the coroner thinks she was killed somewhere else and the body moved to the loading dock."

"Anything about the funeral arrangements? I suppose I should go."

"Nothing yet. I'll let you know. Take care of yourself. It looks like someone doesn't want you there."

"I'll be careful," I said and rang off. There wasn't much to do, and it looked like a good afternoon for a nap.

....

The morning sun was in my eyes as I tried to sleep. It was too early for breakfast, so I made myself a cup of coffee and sat out on the porch and watched the day begin. I had taken a long nap and then turned in early last night. I must have needed the sleep, because today I felt more rested and ready to go. As soon as the breakfast bell rang I was off to the dining room for their huge buffet breakfast. When I returned to the cabin the auto glass repair truck had arrived and the two workers were busy installing my new windshield.

"How long before I can drive it?" I asked.

"As soon as we're finished, give the adhesive about an hour to settle and then you're good to go," said the guy who seemed to be in charge.

"Great!" I said. I took my box lunch into the cabin and packed up my backpack. I would be able to get on the road by ten o'clock.

Beaver Lake has only one general store so that was my first stop of the day. I took out the photo of Bryan Landry and showed it to the clerk.

"Has he been in this store lately?" I asked.

"Not that I remember. He came in here a few times several weeks ago. I remember him because we don't get a lot of strangers here this time of year. But no, he hasn't been in lately."

"If I wanted to buy camping supplies, where around here would I go?" I asked.

"The nearest sporting goods store is in Calais, which is about twenty miles away."

"Thanks," I said. I bought two bottles of water and headed out of town toward Calais. The road to Calais was anything but a highway. In fact it was barely paved. It took me over an hour to cover the twenty miles out of the Maine woods.

Calais lies on the Canadian border and sits on the St. Croix River. Across the river is St. Stephen, New Brunswick. I was able to find the sporting goods store with no problem.

"Have you recently sold a Northern Woods Hiking Dome tent?" I asked the clerk referring to the notes I had taken at the logging camp.

"I sold two last week," he answered. I took out the photo of Bryan Landry and passed it to her.

56

"That's him," she said. "He also bought a sleeping bag, a backpacking stove, and some freeze dried food and a backpack."

"Was there anything unusual about the sale?" I asked.

"Well," she hesitated, "he took everything out of the packaging and packed the backpack up here in the store. It was just like he was leaving from here to go camping."

"Did he have a car?"

"No, he seemed to be on foot."

"What color was the tent?"

"Well, it comes in yellow or blue, but the one he bought was blue. What is this all about?" she asked.

"He's disappeared and we are trying to locate him."

"People go into the Maine woods and have no respect for the dangers," she said.

My last job of the day was to return to the logging camp and check out the campsite. It was pretty clear that the tent and the food had belonged to Bryan Landry. I just hoped this time my windshield wouldn't get smashed out.

I had stopped along the way and consumed the contents of my box lunch and arrived at the logging camp around three in the afternoon. It seemed like a long walk after a busy morning, but I couldn't return home without checking to see if Bryan had returned to the camp. I was hoping that he would think it safe to come back and that maybe I would find him there and get some answers. Of course it didn't work out that way.

There was no sign of the tent, which meant that Bryan had returned to the site and retrieved the tent and

57

moved to another location. At least I could report that Bryan was alive and well, but what on earth was he running from?

It took me a few minutes to see it, but on a tree by the former campsite was a note pinned to the tree. I took it down, unfolded it, and read it.

"I'll be damned," I said as I read it. The note was written in pencil and said: "Stop looking for me or you'll get me killed."

. . . .

A summer-like breeze was blowing through the open office window. Tim was looking at the note I had brought back.

"This here," said Tim, "is what we call a clue."

"A clue to what?" I asked.

"It tells us that Bryan Landry is hiding from something or someone."

"And what do we do with that information?" I asked.

"It depends on what the client wants us to do now. We located his son and discovered that he is in hiding. I'll call Al and give him the facts so far."

"Okay," I answered. "What do you want me to do now?"

"I want you," said Tim with a serious tone, "to go home and get some rest. Derek will be at the museum tonight and then the museum is closed. We are going to take the weekend off. Now go home. I'll be home in a few hours."

I took the hint and harnessed up Argus, who had been sleeping under my desk. I walked out into the street and stopped at Erebus to see Rhonda. The shop was only a few doors down from the Reynolds block.

"Bright blessings!" said Viola Vickner as I walked into the shop. Viola was Rhonda's assistant and resident pagan. She came over and gave me a hug.

"I haven't seen you in weeks!" said Viola. "Sorry to hear about your ex-wife." Viola was wearing a long purple cape over a silver dress, looking every bit the Wiccan practitioner.

"Thanks," I replied. "I really must be in shock. I feel bad that someone died, but I haven't seen her in over twenty years and it's like a stranger died."

"Yes, it must be weird."

"Where's the old lady?" I asked.

"She in the back room, trying to use the computer."

I excused myself and went into the back room of the shop where I found Rhonda hunched over the computer muttering some obscene four-letter words. Argus had stayed behind with Viola, getting as much attention as he could.

"Nice talk!" I said as I slid into the room.

"I can't figure out," said Rhonda with an edge in her voice, "how to make mailing labels with this data base."

"Out of my way," I said and sat down to the computer. In about three minutes I had the labels printing out on the printer. "You had it almost done, you just needed to check this box on the menu."

"This is why I need you back here. So what's up with you?"

"Nothing, I just spent two days at Beaver Lake on a case. Now Tim's ordered me home to rest up. I'm not sure why."

"Everyone is just a little worried about you. You saw your ex-wife's murdered body. It must have had some effect on you."

"Well, to tell the truth, all the memories of college came back to me. All the fun and shared jokes we had back then. But I can't quite reconcile the body on the loading dock as the person I knew all those years ago. It's bothering me that I can't connect."

"That's completely normal," said Rhonda. "It isn't easy to connect the past and the present when there has been a long gap like that."

"I guess," I sighed.

"Go home and get some rest. You look like shit! And the next time I see you there better be a cake in it for me."

I collected Argus and we walked up Center Street to High Street and on home. The lilac bushes were blooming in the yard of Eagle's Nest. I was glad to be home.

Chapter 10

The birds were singing loudly as the sun was coming up. I was trying to go back to sleep and hunkering down into the covers, but Argus was getting restless and jumped on the bed and started to lick my nose. Tim was still sleeping. Tim can sleep through anything and, being a light sleeper, I always resented the way he could drift off without a care. I thought of smacking him in the head, but I thought my day might be ruined by committing murder so early in the day.

"You need to go out?" I asked Argus. He began to bark and went running in circles as I stumbled out of bed. I flipped on the coffee maker as I went past the kitchen and opened the back door to let Argus out. Even though the backyard is fenced in and safe, Argus will not go out unless I go with him. It was a cold morning and I was standing there in just my briefs. I had forgotten to take a robe with me when I headed out of the bedroom. It wasn't a great start to the day.

"It must be Tuesday," I said to Argus as he scrambled back into the house. I hate Tuesdays! They are always the worst day of the week!

"Talking to yourself?" asked Tim. He had gotten up and was sitting at the table in the kitchen. Tim had donned sweat pants and a sweat shirt. "Aren't you cold?"

"Yes to both questions." I went back into the bedroom and put on a heavy robe. When I got back Tim passed me a cup of coffee and sliced up some bread to make toast. I sat down and took a sip of coffee. I watched Tim move around the kitchen. I admired the graceful way he moved around the room.

61

"A little grumpy this morning are we?" he asked.

"Sorry. I didn't sleep well and you know what I'm like before I have my coffee."

"That's for sure!"

I took another sip of coffee as Tim handed me a piece of buttered toast. The coffee was beginning to take effect and my head was clearing up a bit. Argus was on the floor under my feet and watching Tim and me, just in case we decided to drop something on the floor.

"So what's new at the office?" I asked. "You kicked me out yesterday before I could get an update."

"So far we have only the two cases. Bryan Landry's missing person's case and the museum's supposed haunting. We know that Bryan is alive and we know that he is somewhere around Beaver Lake. As to the happenings at the museum, we've established our presence so we can explore without causing alarm or gossip. It seems that the museum is very careful about its image. It wouldn't be good if it were known that it was haunted."

"I would think a murder would be much worse publicity than a rumor of a haunting," I added.

"Yes, but no one is paying us for that and the police are in charge of the murder investigation."

"I know that, but if someone from my past is murdered, I take it personally."

"Well," said Tim slowly. "If we find anything , we can share it with the police. But as far as we are concerned, we are not getting involved!"

"Sure," I agreed. Nothing to stop me from looking around by myself, though.

I had ordered two cords of fire wood to be delivered to the house. Iit would have all summer to dry and season in the summer heat before we would need it in the fall and winter. The truck pulled into the driveway and dumped the load in a pile. I gave the driver a check and then began stacking the wood. Tim came out to help me and we worked quietly and quickly.

"What are you doing tonight?" asked Tim.

"What did you have in mind?" I asked as we stacked the last of the wood.

"Tonight might be a good night to start our investigation at the museum. We can go in after the museum closes and start to debunk the ghost rumors."

"Sounds like fun. Do you actually know what to do?"

"No. You're the one with the ghost hunting background. I thought you would know."

"Okay then. First we need to make a list of what people claim to think they've seen or heard."

"Good. We have that. Bill Baker gave us a list of the reports that he's collected. We have it at the office. We can swing by there and pick it up."

"And we will need an EMF meter."

"What the hell is that?" asked Tim.

"It's a meter that measures electro-magnetic frequencies. It's used by electrical workers to measure electricity leaks. The theory is that spirits use electrical energy to manifest and that we can measure their presence by reading the electrical field."

"You're kidding, right?"

"Not at all. Some people are very sensitive to electrical energy. If there is a high EMF reading in a room, it can make some people feel paranoid. They feel as though someone is watching them. They can even imagine that there is someone there with them. Often the high EMF readings are the result of unshielded electrical wires in the walls."

"Where do we get one of those meters?" asked Tim.

"You can buy them in electrical supply stores. We can probably pick one up one the way to the museum."

"I'm going to call Jessica. She can swing by the office and pick up the reports, then she and Derek can meet us at the museum."

The museum was closed and alarmed when we arrived. I unlocked the staff door and Tim disarmed the alarm. The four of us headed to the conference room to review the files. Jessica handed me the files, and I read the report.

"The activity seems to have started about a year ago. Most of the reports are anecdotal, but some of them have been verified by museum staff members. The cleaning staff reports that they feel as though they are being watched when they are in the European gallery."

"That's hard to prove or disprove," observed Tim.

"Though," began Derek, "I have the same feeling when I'm in the gallery alone."

"We should check to see if there are electrical cables running in the walls of the gallery," I replied. "According to research, high EMF's from electrical wires can create a feeling of paranoia. Some people are more susceptible than others."

"We have the EMF meter," Tim said to Jessica and Derek, "so we can check that theory easily enough."

"The other incidences may be harder to check. According to staff reports from January, security opened up the museum and found one Hudson River painting had been removed from the wall and placed on the floor."

"Could it have just fallen off the wall?" asked Jessica.

"Not according to the curator. The paintings are secured to the wall to prevent such things. The next incident took place in the sculpture gallery. The Zorak was moved. It normally faces out to the gallery, but in February it was found facing the wall. It weighs over sixty pounds."

"Both of these could have been done by a practical joker," observed Tim.

"True enough," I agreed. "Except the fact that security cameras were unable to capture anything. The cameras do a sweep of the gallery, and according to security, everything was normal on the first sweep and then things were moved by the time the cameras did another sweep. Each sweep was less than a minute."

"Do we have copies of the tapes?" asked Derek.

"Yes, we do. We can check them out anytime," answered Tim.

"The next items are more interesting," I continued. "Take a look at these!" I handed out some photos taken by visitors to the museum.

"What am I looking at?" asked Jessica. Before I could answer her she said, "Oh, I see it now. That is spooky!"

The photo showed a happy couple posing at the bottom of the stairs in the main gallery. Just above them on the stairway was the faint image of a woman. The spooky thing about the photo was that she appeared to be transparent."

"Double exposure?" asked Derek.

"Not likely," I answered. "Digital cameras typically don't allow double exposures. Still there might be a logical explanation."

"Such as…?" asked Jessica.

"No idea," I answered. "There's also this one." I handed around the next photo.

"I don't get it." Derek was looking at the photo with a puzzled expression.

"As you can see it's a picture of a visitor and a portrait painting behind her. Notice anything about the painting?"

"The face is kind of spooky looking, but nothing supernatural there."

"Except for the fact," I replied, "that it is a mirror and not a painting." Derek let out a low whistle.

"So we were hired to debunk these happenings. It wouldn't be good for the museum if people began to suspect that it was haunted," said Tim.

"And there is no such thing as ghosts!" proclaimed Derek.

"Don't be so sure," I answered.

Chapter 11

There is something special about night time. The colors of the day have faded and left only gray phantoms, and the air has cooled with even a slight chill. Summer nights in Maine give one a sense of well-being. My sense of well-being was being severely compromised as I was presently standing in the middle of an art gallery holding an EMF meter in my hand watching the meter jump up and down.

"What's going on with that thing?" asked Tim.

"The needle is jumping. There is energy coming from somewhere," I answered.

"Is it a ghost?" asked Jessica in an excited voice.

"There's no such thing!" replied Derek in a stage whisper from across the room.

"Wait until you've been a police officer for a while. You'll see some strange things," said Tim. Tim was a skeptic, but since hooking up with me, he had seen some stuff he couldn't explain.

I continued to walk around the gallery, noting where the energy spikes appeared to be. It was clear that it was all coming from one direction.

"It seems to be coming from this wall," I said as I moved around with the meter. "Derek, would you go into the utility room and turn off the main power switch. Leave it off for about two minutes and then turn it on again."

"Sure thing Jesse," he said as he left the gallery. A few minutes later we were plunged into darkness. Just as I suspected, the meter, which had been showing high EMF readings, settled down to nothing. Tim took advantage of the darkness and maneuvered over to where I was standing and started to grope me in the dark. It was a bold move considering his daughter was only a few feet away. In a few minutes the lights went back on and the EMF's increased. Tim had moved back to his original position.

"I have very good night vision, by the way dad," said Jessica

"Okay," I said to rapidly change the subject. "We've debunked the ghosts in this gallery. There must be a main power line running behind the wall in this room. Anyone who is susceptible to electrical fields is going to feel spooked here. I suggest that we encourage the museum to call in an electrician and have the wires shielded."

"Got it!" said Jessica as she wrote in her notebook. Derek returned to the gallery shortly.

"It's getting late," said Tim. "Let's call it a night."

"Amen to that," replied Jessica, glancing at her father. "Too much testosterone in this place."

....

I was in the break room of the Big Boys' Detective Agency taking blueberry muffins out of the oven and pouring coffee for Jessica and Tim and refreshing my own cup. In the weeks since we had taken over the agency, I hadn't done much cooking. I hadn't quite figured out how to balance my time. Argus had taken a place in the corner and was keeping an eye on me. I reached for a dog treat and he came flying across the room.

"Smells great," observed Jessica as she and Tim came into the break room.

"Is Derek working today?" I asked.

"Yes, he has a double shift today. He left early this morning."

"I never wanted you to get mixed up with a cop," said Tim.

"Give it up old man," replied Jessica. "I'm a grown woman."

"So I've noticed. And you're a stubborn one at that." Jessica just rolled her eyes and grabbed a muffin.

"How are your cookbook sales?" asked Jessica in an attempt to change the subject.

"Slow and steady. I've been getting good reviews," I answered. I had written two cookbooks based on simple recipes I had gleaned from years of researching Maine cooking. The first was a book based on what I called "white trash cooking." It was simple and tasty rural Maine dishes. The second was a vegetarian version of simple to prepare dishes. Rhonda's sister Janet was my book agent. "My agent is encouraging me to come up with a third book, but I have no ideas for a new one."

"You've been using the slow cooker more often since we started the agency. Maybe you could turn that into a cookbook," suggested Tim.

"Not a bad idea actually!" I answered. "I never would have thought of that."

"Glad to help out."

"So what are we doing today?" I asked.

"We have a new client coming in at noon today," said Jessica. "It's a domestic issue of some kind."

"Probably a divorce case," sighed Tim. "But a case is a case."

"I'll be in my office researching the Turner Museum and checking personnel files," I said. I grabbed my coffee cup and headed to my office. Argus came with me trailing behind.

....

The Turner Museum of Art was founded in 1912 by William and Mary Turner. They had spent a lifetime traveling throughout Europe and collecting art of various types. Both of the Turners took the big water bath when the Titanic sank. They were worth millions and left their art collection and mansion for the creation of an art museum. They also left a sizable fortune to help establish and maintain it for the citizens of Maine.

Over the years the museum had been infused with donations and bequests and had grown to be one of the best small museums in New England. A write-up in the *Portland Press Herald* in August 1985 reported that the museum was thought to be haunted. There was no other mention of it in subsequent articles. A Halloween article in *Yankee Magazine* in 1990 listed the Turner Gallery among one of the twenty-five most haunted places in New England. Again there were very few specific details. It was starting to look to me like a publicity stunt. I picked up the phone and called Monica.

"Are you free for lunch?" I asked when she answered the phone.

"What's going on?" she asked.

"I need a psychic detective."

"I'm in," she answered."

"I have a noon appointment, so how around one o'clock at Ruby's?"

"Okay, see you then," and she rang off.

Mrs. Jayne P. Durbin was blonde, slim, and dim. She was well-dressed and sported some expensive jewelry. I guessed her age to be between thirty-five and forty. She sat with her legs crossed and her skirt hiked up as far as it could without actually showing her lady parts. I was tempted to tell her to save the effort, but I wasn't sure she would get it.

"I think my husband is cheating on me," she said as she batted her eyelashes at Tim.

"What makes you think that?" I asked. She looked at me like she had just found half a worm in her apple.

"It's just a feeling I have," she stated somewhat slowly. "He works late one or two times a week. I know he must have a girlfriend. I want you to investigate and catch him."

"We can investigate, but we can't catch him if he isn't doing anything," replied Tim.

"I have money," she said.

I pulled out a contract with our investigation rates. She looked it over and didn't flinch. She pulled out her checkbook and wrote a check and passed it to me.

"Will this be enough for a retainer?" she asked.

I looked at the amount. "That should be fine. Sign here." She signed the contract and left.

"Not the sharpest knife in the drawer," I said.

"We'll be doing her a service by putting her pretty little mind at ease."

"It's a humanitarian move," I replied as I looked at the check.

When I got to Ruby's, Monica was already waiting for me. She had snagged one of the outside tables with a view of the river. Off in the distance we could see the traffic racing over the bridge.

"What a beautiful day," said Monica as I sat down.

"Winter is long and cold, but the payoffs are days like this."

The waiter came over and gave us menus. We both ordered without looking at it. The waiter skipped off to the kitchen.

"They always have unusual people working here," observed Monica as she watched the waiter head off with our orders.

"His name is Jason and he is a friend of Viola's."

"That explains it all! So what's up?"

I explained to her about the museum's reputation as being haunted and gave her a quick rundown about our investigation.

"So you want me to tell you if the museum is really haunted?" she asked.

"Well." I hesitated. "More or less."

"You know as much about haunting and spirits as I do." We had both grown up around people who regularly held séances. We had both become skeptics as we grew up, but we had seen a lot of things that couldn't be explained away.

"Two psychics are better than one," I replied.

"It might be fun. I haven't been to a séance since I was sixteen."

"I remember that one. It was grandma's last one."

"It was quite a show, if I remember correctly!"

"Let's hope this one is a bust. I'd hate to have my skepticism challenged."

"I know what you mean."

Chapter 12

It was just like in the movies. It was raining and we were all dressed in black standing around with umbrellas. The immediate family members were gathered around the grave and the rest of us were standing back at a respectful distance. I had asked Rhonda to go with me, having declined Tim's offer of support. I thought having Tim with me would be too weird, the past and the present colliding.

"Those who are no more," began the Unitarian minister, "are beyond the pain and sorrow of this world. It is up to us, the living to celebrate life and remember that we too, shall pass away into oblivion."

"What the hell type of words of comfort are those?" whispered Rhonda.

"Unitarians," I explained, "are not big believers of the afterlife."

"Is that the husband?" asked Rhonda.

"That is one of her earlier husbands. Her present husband is the one in the tan rain jacket. His name is James Freeman."

"How many husbands did she have?"

"Four," I replied. "Enough to easily qualify for your family!" Rhonda and her sister Janet had several marriages each.

"Asshole!" whispered Rhonda.

"Bite me!" I whispered back. People were beginning to look our way. We both stepped back under the protection of a tree and out of sight.

"I've been asked," said the minister at the conclusion of the service, "to invite everyone back to the church hall for a brief reception in honor of Kelley Kennedy."

74

"You want to go?" asked Rhonda.

"I wouldn't miss it for the world," I replied.

The church hall had twice as many people at the reception as attended the graveside service. People must not have wanted to get wet. There was coffee and freshly baked goodies by the church ladies. A crowd was gathered around James Freeman. I spotted one of her previous husbands off in a corner. I went over to him and introduced myself.

"Hello," I said. "Jesse Ashworth. Husband number one."

"Hi Jesse," he replied looking me over. "Jeff Hastings, husband number three."

"Does this feel weird to you?" I asked. "I haven't seen her in over twenty-five years. It's like she is a fictional character from a book I read once."

"Same for me," replied Jeff. "I haven't seen her for almost twenty years. My only question is why someone hadn't killed her sooner."

"Well," I said. "I never would have said that out loud, but I know exactly what you mean!" Kelley knew how to press one's buttons and made sure she stayed in practice.

"Still," he said. "It's odd to think of her as dead."

"Murdered!" I reminded him.

"Not so odd at all, maybe."

I looked across the room to see Rhonda talking with someone she must have known. Suddenly there were two uniformed police officers at the door, along with what I surmised as two plain clothes officers. The four of them moved up to widower.

"James Freeman," said one of the plain clothes officers. "You are under arrest for the murder of Kelley Kennedy."

Spring was about to turn to summer with an approaching warm front. In anticipation of the change the birds outside the window were raising a ruckus. The sound was coming through the open window in Tim's office. Alan Landry, Tim, Jessica and I were seated at the little conference table. Argus had taken his position in Jessica's lap and was watching the conversation.

"So you have no idea what type of trouble Bryan could be in?" asked Tim.

"No!" replied Al. I could tell that the disappearance of his son was having an effect on him. "Do you think he is in danger?"

"The note," I replied, "was warning me off and hinted that if I continued looking for him, that it would not be in his best interest."

"I don't understand!" Al shook his head. "One moment he was working at the museum and taking art lessons, and the next he runs away."

"Art lessons?" Tim looked up from the file he had in front of him. "This is the first I've heard of art lessons."

"He was taking two graduate art courses at the university. I don't see how it is relevant."

"Well, it may be unrelated, but we should look into his art classes. Anything else you forgot to tell us?" Tim seemed a little annoyed.

Alan Landry wrote us a check for our work so far and asked us to continue looking into Bryan's disappearance. I reminded him that there was no guarantee that we could find him. We shook hands and he left.

"An ex-cop should know better that to leave out information, no matter how unrelated he thinks it is." Tim just shook his head.

"So where are we?" I asked.

"We have three active cases," Tim reminded me. "Bryan Landry's disappearance, the museum investigation, and Jayne Durbin's straying husband."

"And the dozen security systems that we monitor," I added. "They are our steady income-producing jobs. Jessica, could you make up an advertisement for security systems?" I asked. "It's something that we could expand on. Mr. Boyce and Mr. Bigg really hadn't done much expansion in the last few years."

"I'll get right on it Jesse." She lifted Argus off her lap, set him down, and went back to her desk.

"You want to take the first shift of surveillance and tail the cheating Mr. Durbin?"

"Actually Monica and I are going to the museum tonight and check for ghosts."

"You're having a séance? I'd love to be there!" Tim laughed.

"If anything happened during the séance you would be scared shitless!"

"I could handle it."

"I got something you can handle," I said.

Tim just nodded and smiled. "Later guy!"

It was windy and warm and the air was humid. It felt more like July and not late May. I also knew that within

77

hours we could be plunged into forty degree weather. The only constant to Maine weather was its changeability. It was a quiet night; it was too late in the season for spring peepers and too soon for crickets. There was no moon visible and the stars were shining brightly in the night sky.

I swiped my key card and stepped through the museum door. Monica was close behind me. I entered the code in the key pad and disarmed the security system. I flipped on the light and we headed to the security office.

"This might not be all that great an idea," sighed Monica as she took a seat.

"Getting cold feet?"

"No, but you have to admit it is kind of spooky here."

I reached into the closet and found two flashlights. "Of course it's spooky here. Imagine all the emotional energy that goes into a painting. Anyone with any sensitivity can feel that."

"What are we doing first?" she asked.

"Using the security cameras we'll take some still shots in the galleries. Then when we are done we'll repeat the procedure. After the séance, we'll come back here and review the surveillance tapes."

"You mean our séance is going to be on tape?"

"The tape might get erased," I added, "if we look too stupid. And I have this digital recorder to use during the séance. It may pick up any activity that we are unable to hear. The theory is that spirits are able to manipulate electrical devices and can produce voice imprints that we cannot hear."

"Yes, I know. It's called electronic voice phenomenon or EVP's."

"Some of the findings have been impressive, and" I added, "spooky! A Norwegian bird watcher was recording bird songs in 1959. When he played the tape back later he was shocked to discover a voice commenting on the birds. Skeptics believe that EVP's are just recording random CB and radio broadcasts. Others think that EVP's are really the voices of the dead."

"And what do *you* think?" Monica was testing me.

"I think they are interesting."

We set up a table in the middle of the main gallery. All the lights were out and we used our flashlights to find our way around. The movement of the flashlights created shadows that seemed to move with us as we circulated around the area. In this atmosphere I could imagine that people's minds could easily play tricks on them. Monica and I, having been brought up in an occult-leaning family, weren't as easily influenced.

"I'm not seeing anything unusual," I said as I swept the gallery with my flashlight.

"Me either."

We took our seats at the table and turned off our flashlights. Except for the red glowing exit signs, we were in the dark.

"I feel a little bit foolish," I said as I turned on the recorder and took out the EMF meter and turned it on.

"It has been a few years. I keep telling myself that it's all a bunch of hooey, but it really doesn't feel that way. You know what I mean?"

"Yes, my rational mind is sometimes at war with my more primitive instincts."

79

I took a deep breath. "Is there anyone here who wants to say something?"

"Please make your presence known," whispered Monica. Nothing happened.

"Let's just clear our minds and try to meditate and see what happens." We were quiet and off in the distance we heard the sound of something moving.

"If that was you," said Monica, "would you do that again?" We listened carefully and we heard another faint sound.

"I was hoping that wouldn't happen," I whispered.

"Just the building settling, I hope."

"Shit!" I said. The EMF meter's light was flickering. "There shouldn't be any electrical readings in here. I turned off all electricity in the gallery." The light continued to flicker.

"Let's see if it responds to questions."

"Are you the one who keeps moving things here?" The light stopped flickering.

"Is there someone else here? Just move toward the meter and it will light up. One flash for no and two flashes for yes." I felt foolish speaking to the empty gallery. The light flashed three times. Monica and I took turns asking questions.

"Are you alone?" asked Monica. One flash.

"Is there someone else here?" Two flashes.

'How many of you are here?" Three flashes.

"So there are three of you?" Two flashes.

"Do you have a reason to be here?" The lights began flashing and then stopped. All subsequent questions went unanswered.

"I think Casper has taken a powder," I whispered. I got up, took the flashlight, found the light switches and the gallery was flooded with light. I walked around the gallery with the EMF meter to see if there was any unusual electro-magnetic activity, but neither the needle nor the lights showed anything unusual.

"What do you make of all this?" asked Monica.

"Well, if I were a member of a TV ghost hunting team, I'd get all excited for the camera. However, in real life I'm sure there is a logical explanation, like sunspots, radio interference, something like that."

"So basically," said Tim later that night as he was rubbing the tension away in my neck and shoulders, "you saw some flashing lights and heard some noises and that was it?"

"I also checked the video cameras and didn't see anything. And if you keep that up," I said referring to the shoulder and neck rub, "I might have to keep you around."

"I'm counting on that."

Chapter 13

Sometime during the night a warm air mass slid into New England. When I woke up I could feel the change in the air. Argus jumped up and ran for the door. I stumbled out of bed and left Tim sleeping. Argus could never figure out what he should do first, go outside and do his business, or attack a bowl of kibble. As usual he went for the dog food and then rushed out the door just in time. I put on a pot of coffee and checked the freezer for some frozen waffles.

"What's for breakfast?" asked Tim as he strode into the kitchen wearing only white boxer briefs.

"Well, there doesn't seem to be much in the house. The emergency supply of waffles is running low." Tim was teasing me. He knows I hate making breakfast.

"Considering all the work you did last night," he said with a smile, "both at the museum and at home, I'll treat you to breakfast. I think we're going to have a long day at the office." He poured out two cups of coffee and sat at the table.

"In that case, I'll walk to work with Argus and you can stop at Ruby's and pick up breakfast and bring it to the office. I thought when we took on the agency, we wouldn't be working all that hard. What's up with that?"

"We only have three cases, plus the security alarms. As soon as we can solve them, we'll be done."

"Okay," I answered. I couldn't quite see how any of those cases was going to be solved anytime soon.

When I first retired from teaching and bought Eagle's Nest, it was a rundown bungalow with overgrown weeds. This morning it was a neat and tidy little house with a colorful garden. All four houses on the street were neat and tidy. My elderly neighbors, the Lowells, were out sitting on their front porch sipping coffee. I gave them a wave as I passed by. Rabbi Beth White had already left for work, and there seemed to be no one living in the Wilson house. I'd have to check with the Lowells to get the scoop on that.

It took Argus and me about twenty minutes to reach the office. Tim arrived several minutes later with breakfast sandwiches. Jessica wasn't due in for another hour, so I checked for messages. There were none.

"So where are we?" I asked Tim as we sat down with coffee and breakfast.

"Derek is checking out our security customers as time allows. Jessica is working on an advertisement for our alarm and security services. The Bryan Landry case is on hold until something new comes in, and Derek shadowed the cheating husband last night. So we should get a report when he comes in later this morning, and since I doubt the museum is really haunted, we should be able to wrap that up in a few days."

"What about Kelley Kennedy's murder? We were the ones who found the body."

"No one is paying us for that, and did you forget that they arrested the husband?"

"Do you think he did it?" I asked.

"I think the police think he did. And it's really not our business."

"I suppose you're right," I replied. It wouldn't hurt for me to ask a few questions on my own would it? No reason to share that with the big guy right now, though.

83

"It was a boring job," complained Derek. "I followed James Durbin, AKA the cheating husband, for three hours. First he left work and went to the gym for a workout, then he stopped off at Billy's Sports Bar. I followed him inside. By the way, I'm putting the beer on my expense account. I couldn't just sit there and watch him empty handed now could I?"

"Just keep your receipts," I said. "Did he talk to anyone there?"

"Just the bartender. Then he got in his car and drove home."

"Well, the goodwife paid us to watch him," said Tim. "So we'll watch him for a few days and then give her a written report. Jesse can do tonight's surveillance, and I'll do tomorrow night's stake out."

"Sure thing," I agreed.

"Well." said Derek, "I need to get back to my real job as one of Bath's finest. I have to work the day shift today."

My desk was covered with files of the three cases we were working on. I was getting frustrated with the lack of progress. I'm the type who wants to get things done as soon as possible, and having open files on my desk just doesn't make me happy.

"Someone to see you Jesse," said Jessica as she poked her head into my office.

"Well, send them in." I tidied up the stack of files and moved them to the far corner of my desk.

"Hi Jesse! Remember me, Jeff Hastings," said the man as he took a seat across from my desk.

"Kelley's number three husband, if I remember correctly."

"Yes, we are members of a small, but diverse club."

"What can I do for you Jeff?"

"It's about Kelley's death. I know this is going to sound strange, but James Freeman and I are friends."

It took me a minute to take it in. "You are husband number three and you are friends with the present husband?"

"I told you it would sound strange, but yes, we are friends. Kelley and I were a long time divorced before Jim met and married her."

"And how did you meet him?" I asked. This was getting to be a little weird.

"We have been friends from college. He had never met Kelley when we were married. So imagine the surprises all around when he introduced me to his fiancée."

I had to laugh. I could just picture it in my mind. Kelley always planned the outcomes in advance and didn't like surprises. This would have sent her into apoplexy!

"So what can I do for you?" I asked.

"I don't think Jim killed her. I think the police have the wrong guy."

"The police seem to think he did it."

"They've got the wrong guy. I want you to investigate."

"What if I find out he's guilty?"

"You won't." I pulled out our rate sheet and contract papers and pushed them toward him. He looked them over, wrote a check and then stood up to shake my hand.

"I'll go see him tomorrow," I assured him.

I was flipping through the files on my desk and not making much progress. I was about to fling them across the room in frustration when Tim came running into my office.

"You are not going to believe this!"

"Don't be too sure," I answered. "I've had an unbelievable morning already." Jessica followed her father into the room when she heard the tone of his voice.

"What is it?" she asked.

"I just got a call from the museum. They found another body on the loading dock."

"What!" screamed Jessica.

"Who is it?" I asked.

"Janet Costa. She was an outside auditor, hired to look at the museums books."

"That place has bad karma," I said.

"At least it has nothing to do with our cases," Tim said.

"Actually Tim, it might." I told him about taking on Jim Freeman's case, and how a new murder might impact it.

Tim just sat down and sighed, "I need to retire for real."

When we arrived at the museum they were just taking the body away on a stretcher. I was grateful for two things: first the body was covered and second was the fact that I hadn't made the discovery. James Baker was pacing back and forth and wringing his hands.

"What happened?" asked Tim.

"A delivery truck pulled up to the loading dock around noon and made the discovery. As far as I know

86

she was in the bookkeeper's office working this morning."

"What about camera surveillance?" I asked.

"That's just the problem. We were having the system serviced. We figured daytime was the best time to have the system down. We had plenty of security guards on hand today."

"But no one saw anything?" asked Tim.

"No, they didn't. The police are questioning them now, so maybe they can shake something loose."

One of the plain clothes detectives joined us after the coroner's people took the body away.

"How is it," asked Jacob Wright, "that there have been two murders at the museum, and you two have turned up for both?" Jacob Wright was the detective who had investigated Kelley's murder.

"Good timing," I answered.

"We're doing security work for the museum," added Tim.

"Not a very good job. Two dead bodies!"

"This should clear Jim Freeman. He's in jail, so he couldn't have done this murder," I said thinking of my new client.

"We don't know that the two are related. This could just be a copycat. There are several differences in the murder scene," added Detective Wright.

"Such as?" asked Tim.

"Kelley Kennedy died of severe head trauma; Janet Costa was strangled, as far as we can tell. The coroner can confirm the cause of death. Kelley Kennedy was dressed up for the murder. The Costa woman was in her street clothes."

"At least," I added, "we know that Jim Freeman didn't do this one."

87

Sagadahoc County in Maine has too little crime to support a county jail, so they partnered with Lincoln county and built one county jail called Two Bridges Regional Jail and it is located just off route one in Wiscasset. It was a perfect day weather wise, and I rode to the jail with the sunroof open and the windows down. I had arranged to meet Jim Freeman and hear what he had to say. Jeff Hastings was convinced that Jim hadn't killed Kelley. I wasn't so sure.

A guard led me into a room that looked like a cafeteria. Little tables were spread around the room and people were sitting at a few of them. The prisoners were easy to identify in their orange jumpsuits. Another guard brought Jim to the table where I was sitting. I got up, we shook hands and the guards moved off to survey the room.

"Jeff told me that he hired you to help me."

"Yes, he did, though I'm not sure how much help I can be."

"Anything will be helpful at this point. They think I killed Kelley."

"Okay," I began. "Tell me what happened and why the police think you killed Kelley."

"Kelley had planned to go away for a few days. She was studying art and told me she wanted to concentrate on her art and paint."

"Kelley was an artist?" I asked. This was news to me. When I knew Kelley she just drifted from one thing to another and never finished anything. As far as I knew the only talent she had was a sharp tongue.

"As you know Kelley had a few major issues. I'm sure when you knew her she was a real bitch. In recent years she had therapy and medication and was turning her life around. She wasn't a good painter, but she loved to paint and it was something she stuck with."

"I see." Of course I didn't see at all.

"So how long had she been gone?"

"She had been gone for two days and wasn't due back for another day."

"Do you know where she was going?"

"All she said was it was a cabin in the northern woods. If I wanted to get hold of her I was to try her cell phone, though she didn't know if there would be cell service in the area."

"Did she give a location, anything beyond just saying the northern woods?"

"No, but I do know she had a friend who had a cabin on Beaver Lake and I just assumed she was going there.

"Beaver Lake?" Something clicked in my head. Could there be a connection?

"Who did she know in Beaver Lake?"

"Karen Carlson. She and Kelley were best friends and I knew Karen was still in Florida."

"I see." Karen Carlson was one of Bryan Landry's contacts at Beaver Lake. We had dismissed Karen in our investigation of Bryan's disappearance because she was in Florida. My mind was busy trying to fit the two events together, but I wasn't having much luck. Maybe it was just a coincidence.

"So I guess the next question would be where were you during all this time?"

"That's just it. I don't have an alibi. I was home enjoying some time to myself. I didn't see anyone for two days. It wasn't until the police showed up and told me what happened that I had any idea she was dead."

"Do you have any ideas as to why she was at the museum and why she was dressed up as a majorette?"

"She worked at the museum, so being at the museum was not unusual, but I've no idea why she was dressed up as a majorette."

"Are you familiar with the stolen painting called *The Majorette*? "It's been suggested that she was dressed in the same fashion as the painting."

"No idea. I don't know anything about this and I didn't kill her."

"So what motive do the police think you have?"

"They think we had a fight and I killed her for the insurance money."

"How much insurance did she have?"

"About one hundred fifty thousand dollars."

"Well, it could be a motive," I said. "But it's not a great motive. I'm sure they haven't told you yet, but there's been another murder on the loading dock of the museum. And since you were locked up in here; it couldn't have been you. I'm sure your lawyer will have you out of here by the end of the day."

As luck would have it Jim's lawyer was arriving just as I got up to leave. Jim would be home in a matter of hours.

Chapter 14

May was about to slip into June and the official beginning of the summer season was Memorial Day weekend. Almost every Memorial Day that I can remember it has rained, but this year the weather people predicted a sunny and warm holiday. Tim and I were planning a cookout. It would be a good time to catch up with everyone. We had been so busy with the new business that we didn't have as much time as we would like to spend with our friends.

The Memorial Day parade was going to start at the war memorial in front of the courthouse, march through town, and end up in the park where the Navy Band would be performing in the bandstand. After the parade we all planned to head back to Eagle's Nest for the cookout.

Argus knew something was up as Tim and I rushed around in the morning setting things up. Argus loves a parade, and I think he sensed an adventure. He loves the smells and the motion of the parade and sits on the curb mesmerized.

I was busy in the kitchen finishing up several side dishes like macaroni salad and couscous salad to go with the burgers and hot dogs that Tim would be cooking on the grill. I had the homemade baked beans warming up in the crock pot. I wanted to make sure there was plenty to eat for the friends who were vegetarians or semi-vegetarians.

Finally we got in Tim's car and headed to the park. From there we walked up the hill to the court house and joined the crowd waiting for the parade to begin. Off in the distance we could hear the school bands begin playing.

The parade was a cross section of small town life. We had the boy and girl scouts of all ages, the elder veterans, the school and municipal bands, civic organizations, and finally with the biggest cheers came the active duty soldiers who were home on leave. We followed the parade down the hill to the park for the laying of the wreath at the war memorial. In the bandstand the Navy Band played. Argus watched all this with his tail wagging whenever he saw movement.

Tim and I slipped away to get ready for our guests, as people would be arriving soon. Tables were set up in the yard, and I had purchased plenty of red, white, and blue plates and cups and decorations from a party store in Portland. The ice chest was full of beer and soda, the burger patties were made, and everything was ready.

Billy Simpson was the first to arrive. Billy had just finished up a rough time with a divorce and a stretch in rehab, but he was doing great. He had retired from his old job and was now working part time for the library. It was a job he loved.

"Bright Blessings, everyone!" cried Viola Vickner. Today she was dressed in a black monk's robe, silver pentagram, and walking stick.

"You really look like the archetypal witch today," I said.

"Thanks, I figured this cookout could use some magic!" I watched as Viola walked the four corners of the yard and uttered blessings to the four directions.

"There'll be a surprise news item at the end of the party," she said mysteriously. I must have looked worried because she added, "It will be good news, don't worry!"

My neighbors Beth White and John and Dorothy Lowell came over together, grabbed some drinks and settled into the group of lawn chairs under the shade tree.

Rhonda Shepard and Jackson Bennett arrived bringing the makings of gin and tonics. "Make mine a double," I said as I sent them over to the makeshift bar I had set up using an old wooden ironing board that I found in my garage. Rhonda was wearing a 1940's polka dot sun dress with a matching hat, looking very much like Joan Crawford. I suppressed my comment about wire hangers.

The last to arrive was my cousin Monica and best friend Jason, followed by Jessica and Derek. I hadn't seen Jason nearly enough since Tim and I started the agency.

"Viola says there'll be some interesting announcements at the end of the party. Do you have a reading on that?" I asked Monica.

"Oh, yes," she answered mysteriously and wandered off to join the others under the shade tree.

Tim and I joined the others for a drink under the tree to catch up on small town gossip. Argus had the run of the yard and was trying out different laps to see which one he liked best. Tim looked at his watch and headed over to the grill and started to throw food on the glowing coals. I went into the kitchen and brought out the side dishes and set up the buffet.

"Food's ready!" yelled Tim. As usually happens, no one wanted to be the first to line up, so everyone just stayed where they were. "Hey!" yelled Tim when nobody got up. Derek, being the youngest

93

male present and always hungry, finally got up and headed to the food table. Everyone else followed, filled their plates, and headed back to their seats. Rabbi Beth gave a nice, secular blessing, and we began to eat.

After we all had seconds and a little resting time, I went into the kitchen and whipped some cream, brought out the biscuits that I had make earlier, and grabbed a bowl of cut-up strawberries. It was while we were eating the strawberry shortcake that Viola's prediction came true.

"I have some good news to share," announced Jessica. "Derek and I are engaged to be married!"

Everyone wished the couple well and the cookout ended on a celebratory note. Tim, I thought, looked a little pale!

....

"What the fuck is this?" I asked as I stared at the box on my desk.

"It's for protection. You need to learn how to use it," answered Tim. I carefully picked the gun out of the box. "I'm going to take you to the shooting gallery and have an instructor teach you to protect yourself."

"What do I need a gun for?"

"You're a detective now. Every detective has a gun." Actually I was picturing myself with a cool shoulder holster bulging under my jacket, just enough to scare people. Maybe I could get a cool hat and look like Sam Spade. If nothing else a gun would make a great fashion accessory.

"I have no idea how to shoot one. Are you going to teach me?"

"Absolutely not! I don't want to get shot by your bad aim. Better to pay someone else to take that risk."

"Asshole!" I muttered.

Before Tim could utter a response Jessica came into the office and sat at her desk. Actually she more or less had floated into the room. Being engaged seemed to suite her.

"Are you sure you want to get married?" asked Tim. "You're young and there is no hurry!"

Jessica just stared at him and said nothing.

"Don't make me use this gun," I said to Tim. "Your little girl is all grown up and has the right to be happy." I went and stood beside Jessica.

"You're right," admitted Tim. "I just want you to be happy." Jessica ran over to him to give him a hug. Then she came over to me and gave me one.

"You two dads are the best," she said. We all looked at each other for a second and then returned to work.

I went back to to my office and stared at the files on my desk. I picked up Bryan Landry's file and remembered the art class his father had mentioned. I wasn't sure what type of the art class he would have taken, but since Bryan was a student at the university, I thought I would start there,

I pulled up the university's web site to check out the faculty and staff directory. Just as I suspected, Helen Buckley was still working in the registrar's office. Helen and I had been friends in college when we were attending Southern Maine. She had gone to work in the registrar's office after graduation and had worked her way up to the head position. I decided to give her a call.

95

Getting through to an executive is not easy. They do not answer their own phones. After convincing the office gatekeepers that Helen and I were old friends, I was put through. We spent the first five minutes on the phone catching up and promising to meet for lunch soon. Then I explained what I wanted.

"I'm investigating a missing person. He was a student at Southern Maine. I know he took an art class last January, but I'm not even sure where it was, but I thought I'd start here." I gave her the name.

"I can check to see if he enrolled in any courses in January," she offered.

"Actually, if you find that he did, could you sent me the class list?"

"That would be highly irregular," replied Helen in her professional voice.

"I'll keep the list confidential," I promised. "I'm just trying to find Bryan for his own safety." It was mostly true. I did have that mysterious note from Bryan that hinted that he was in danger.

"Okay," I heard Helen's voice slip back into friend mode. "If I find anything I'll send it along. What's your fax number?"

I gave her the number, we set up a date for lunch and I rang off.

Tim poked his head into my office. "Let's go to lunch,"

"Sure thing," I replied. "Where to?"

"I thought we could go home for lunch."

"But there's no food at home."

"I know," answered Tim. It took me a moment to catch on.

"Oh, I get it!" I said.

Chapter 15

Rain fell for several days. The month of June alternates between warm and sunny days of paradise-like jewels and rainy, cold, dreary days when one has to bundle up in sweaters and raincoats and wait for better times. Mainers are aware of the fickle nature of June and plan their vacations for July and August. People from away often come to Maine in June and have to deal with the inclement weather. Today the town was crowded with people shopping and eating in town, since the beaches and campground were soaked in rain and socked in with fog.

For obvious reasons I chose to drive to work instead of walking the mile and a half from Eagle's Nest. I carried Argus into the office in order to keep his paws dry. Argus never minded being carried, especially in the rain.

I checked the fax machine, but there was nothing waiting for me. I guessed that Helen had hit a blank wall when she checked to see if Bryan had taken an art course at the university. Tim had gotten to the office early to get a head start on the day. I had stayed behind and put the evening's meal in the crock pot. I had prepared chicken cordon-bleu. It was one of the best slow cooker recipes I had. I poked my head into Tim's office.

"What's up, Boss?"

"I was just going over the museum investigation. We need to get a handle on whatever is happening there. In addition to the two murders, there is still the unresolved issue of strange happenings."

"The police are in charge of the murders," I said, stating the obvious.

"My experience tells me that sometimes things are related. But you're right, we are not in charge of the murders, but we are being paid to check out security and find out why people think the museum is haunted."

"When are we going back?"

"Tomorrow night. You, me, and Derek are scheduled to be the security team. We need to wrap this case up. Tonight it's your turn to check out this Durbin character. So far Derek and I have seen nothing. He goes to work, goes to the gym, and then Billy's Sports Bar. No evidence of cheating. I'd like to wrap up this case by Friday and have a report for the blonde wife."

"Okay. I'll go home for an early dinner, then I'll be at Durbin's work place when he gets out. By the way, dinner will be in the crock pot when you get home. I'll put it on warm since we won't be eating together."

I had an idea about the museum. As soon as Jessica came in to the office, I left Argus with her, grabbed my rain slicker, and headed out the door. Erebus was just down the street. Since it was too early for the store to be open, I entered through the back door. Rhonda was setting up the cash drawer, and Viola was dusting off the shelves.

"I need a favor," I said as they looked up from their tasks.

"What is it?" asked Rhonda.

"I need you to give Viola the day off."

"What?"

"I'd like her to go and check out the Turner Art Museum."

"Who's paying for that?" asked Rhonda.

"It's official business. The agency will reimburse you."

"Okay," said Rhonda. "You better fill me in on this. It sounds pretty strange."

I tried to explain as best I could. "Viola is a Pagan. By that I mean she is more open to feelings and atmosphere than most of us. I just would like her to go to the museum, like any other visitor, and tell me her impressions of the museum space."

"I'll do that," replied Viola. "I'm well-attuned to vibrations and such."

"And what is this all about?" asked Rhonda.

"All I can tell you is that it's related to a case we are working on."

"Does it have anything to do with the two murders at the museum?" Rhonda asked.

"Not directly, no," I answered evasively.

"Okay with me if Viola is willing to go."

"I'd be glad to go," she answered.

"Keep track of your mileage so we can reimburse you for it. And thanks!"

Durbin usually leaves his office around five-thirty, so I went home around four, scooped out a chicken breast from the crock pot and flipped the device on warm for Tim when he got home. I sat on the back porch with my chicken and a glass of wine and tried to relax. There was nothing exciting about doing surveillance. Usually it's sitting around for hours waiting for something to happen. Argus was stretched out on the floor napping. I really wanted to stay home, but duty called. I finished my dinner, put my dishes in the dishwasher, and put Argus in his crate. Tim would be home in less than an hour to rescue him.

I took the beat up Corolla and drove to Brunswick and waited for Durbin to emerge from the

Bath Iron Works building where he worked. Fortunately it was one of BIW's smaller facilities, so it was less likely that I would lose him in the quitting time traffic.

I spotted Durbin's car as it emerged from the parking lot. I pulled out into the line of traffic a few cars behind him so as not to be spotted. I was pretty sure that he had no idea that he was being investigated. Derek and Tim were both professionals and knew how to tail a suspect. I was just hoping I wouldn't be spotted as this was my first tail!

I followed Durbin's car to the gym. I parked in the large parking lot where I could keep watch, pulled out my M3p player and listened to a book on tape. It was better than just sitting around. After what seemed like an eternity, Durbin emerged from the gym and got in his car.

I expected he would be heading to Billy's Sports Bar as he had on previous nights, but when he left the parking lot he turned his car in the opposite direction. Durbin's car merged onto the interstate and headed south on interstate 295. At the Freeport exit he turned off the highway and headed into Freeport village. It was high tourist season so I was able to follow and blend in with the other traffic.

There were three cars in front of me and I was afraid that I might lose him when one of the cars decided to take a left turn and wait until the traffic was clear in both directions for three miles. I was beginning to panic when I saw Durbin pull into one of L.L. Bean's parking lots. L.L. Bean is a world famous sporting goods and clothing store with a substantial mail order business. The store is open twenty-four hours a day, every day of the year. It's a great place to go, no matter what the time is.

100

Durbin was already out of his car by the time I pulled into the parking lot. So he was going shopping? So what? Nothing illegal or immoral about shopping. I put on my glasses and a hat as a sort of disguise and followed him into the store. Even though it was early evening the store was crowded. L. L. Bean is, after all, open twenty-four hours a day and legend says that the doors have no locks because the doors are never locked. I'd have to check that out one day.

I followed Durbin upstairs, trying to be inconspicuous by stopping ever few feet and pretending to look at merchandise. Fortunately the store was designed with an open concept floor plan and I was able to keep an eye on him from a safe distance away. Durbin went straight for the café, bought a cup of coffee and took a seat at one of the small tables.

I was thinking that Freeport was a little far to go just for a cup of coffee when a trim woman in a business suit sat down at his table. Maybe there was something to his wife's suspicions. As they had just sat down, I figured it would be a good time for me to go to the bathroom. I usually can go no more than two hours at a stretch, and it had already been about four. They seemed settled enough, so I left them there with their coffee.

I swear I was only gone for two minutes, but of course when I got back to the café, they were gone. I raced to the parking lot only to discover that Durbin's car was gone. Who moves that fast?

I took out my cell phone and sent a text to Tim about what happened. Call me a coward, but not all news is better given in person!

....

101

It was a humid morning and the sun was bright red as it appeared over the horizon. My experience told me it was going to be a hot summer day, even though the official date of the beginning of summer was still a few weeks away. Tim had gone into work earlier, and I stayed behind to get caught up on some housework. Argus was following me around as I was dusting, but I'd have to put him in his crate when I got out the vacuum cleaner. I don't know what it is, but dogs hate vacuum cleaners. I was planning to go into work mid-morning and write up my report from last night. I was scheduled to have lunch with Monica and Viola to learn what Viola's impressions of the museum were.

I have a love-hate relationship with housework. I love the fact that when I'm done with it, it really makes a visual difference, but I hate starting it. I'm okay once I get going, but I try to delay it as much as possible. When I finished I made a cup of coffee and sat out on the back porch to enjoy the morning. Argus jumped on one of the chairs and made himself comfortable. I was having trouble motivating myself to go into the office, so I compromised and typed out my report on my laptop while enjoying the quiet of the backyard. When I finished my report I emailed it to the office, along with a note to Tim that I wouldn't be coming into the office today due to a lack of interest. It wasn't that I was really lacking interest, but just feeling overwhelmed with the workload. I'm not a natural multitasker and having more than one case to work on was fracturing my focus.

I did assure Tim that I would be ready for my security shift at the museum this evening, so I really didn't feel that guilty about playing hooky. After my second cup of coffee and a short rest, I put Argus in his crate and drove down to Ruby's for lunch with Monica and Viola. Ruby's outdoor deck was in full swing and I snagged a table with a great water view. I was the first to arrive and ordered a beer. Monica and Viola joined me shortly and we ordered lunch.

"So, what were your impressions of the museum?" I asked Viola after we had exchanged all the small talk. I could tell that Monica was watching Viola for subtle signs and body language. Monica was gifted with the ability to read people.

"I knew that there had been two murders at the museum, so it was hard to discount that knowledge, but I tried. I didn't have the feeling that anyone was killed in the museum, but I do feel that there is something very wrong there."

"Such as?" asked Monica.

"Well, I just felt very uncomfortable in the main gallery." That was pretty much what we knew and probably could be traced to the unshielded electrical cables. "But there is evil there, though more likely related to a person than to any supernatural elements."

"There is some strange energy from some of the paintings," added Monica.

"True," agreed Viola. "I just have to say that I felt very uncomfortable there."

After we finished lunch, Viola excused herself and returned to Erebus. I turned to Monica, "Well?" I asked.

"I think she's not telling us the whole truth. I think she was very uncomfortable at the museum, but didn't want us to think she was in over her head."

"Explain!"

"As a self-proclaimed witch, she takes pride on being in touch with the natural forces of nature. I think

103

she was frightened by what she felt there, but had no frame of reference to explain it to us."

"Well, at least it confirms what we felt there when we did the séance," I added.

"Oh, yes. I have the feeling that you are going to have a very interesting evening there tonight!"

....

Tim stopped on his way home and picked up a large vegetarian pizza. I told him that I could only do one domestic task a day, so since I had cleaned the house, I wasn't going to be cooking dinner.

"What's with you today?" asked Tim. He put the pizza box on the table and opened two beers. "You seem a bit cranky."

"Sorry. I'm just a bit discouraged. I'm used to getting things done, and I haven't been able to make any progress on any of these cases."

"You have to be patient. Things happen in their own time. Investigations take time because you have to always chip away at things. We are very close to solving one or two of these cases now. Just hang in there."

"If you say so," I replied, not really convinced.

Tim, Derek, and I got to the museum about an hour after it had closed for the day. Tim disabled the alarm, and I disabled the security cameras. We were planning an in-depth search of the museum, and we didn't need a video record of our search. I was afraid that someone might view the video and our cover would be blown. To the museum staff we were just three part-time security officers.

"So what are we looking for?" asked Derek.

"We know that things get moved around in the galleries and no one seems to know why. We are looking at everything. We are looking at how the art work is mounted, how secure things seem to be. We are looking for anything that doesn't belong or anything out of place. In other words, look at everything !" answered Tim as he switched on the main light circuits. "I'll start in the west gallery, Jesse, you start upstairs, and Derek, you search the east gallery. And take a flashlight and shine it into every corner and closet in the place."

I headed up the staircase. As I was going up it occurred to me that there must be a space under the stair case. I picked up the radio. "Tim, is there storage space under the stairs?"

"I'll go check," answered Tim. "I don't recall seeing a door."

I continued to the upper gallery. During the day, the upper gallery was filled with filtered daylight. At night the gallery seemed shadowy and spooky. I could understand why some people thought it was haunted. There were several nineteenth century marble statues and in the artificial light they seemed to glow. I walked slowly around the main gallery shining my flashlight into all the dark corners. My radio crackled and Tim spoke.

"There is a small utility door under the stairs. I took the door off and stuck my head in. All that is under the stairs are air conditioning ducts."

"Copy that," I said. Air ducts? Maybe I should check air ducts. It's possible that air flow could be responsible for some of the strange noises.

Off the main gallery was another room called the east gallery. It was smaller than the other galleries

105

and contained the Turner's collection of Impressionist art. Near the floor was a louvered air conditioner vent with the louvers facing down toward the floor. I took out my jack knife and carefully pried off the louvered cover. I aimed my flashlight into the dark vent. Something caught my eye and I reached in and pulled out what looked like a pile of rags. There was something wrapped up in it, and I began to unwrap the object. My heart was pounding. Once I was able to peek inside I grabbed the radio.

"Tim, Derek! I need you up here in the Impressionist gallery now!"

Chapter 16

The earth seemed to be bursting with life. Everything was in bloom. The sunny days and the occasional showers had conspired to make one of the most beautiful Junes on record. My irises were blooming and the colors were more vibrant than I'd ever seen. The only problem with irises is the short season for blooms.

Downtown Bath was gearing up for the tourist season. In a few weeks it would be the Fourth of July, complete with marching bands and majorettes. I was looking into the face of a majorette as I unwrapped the bundle of rags I had just removed from the air conditioner vent.

"That's the stolen painting!" exclaimed Derek as he looked over my shoulder and stated the obvious.

"It never made it out of the museum," added Tim.

"The thief must have hidden it here and expected to retrieve it later," I said as I continued to unwrap the painting.

"This could very easily be an inside job," observed Tim. "A run-of-the-mill thief would have taken it with him and not risked coming back to the museum."

"But who?" I asked.

"That's something we need to find out. There's more going on in this museum than just a few miscellaneous ghosts," said Tim.

....

The next day was sunny and warm with a slight breeze. I told Tim I was taking another day off. I'd had enough of the forty hour work week. The whole idea of having our own agency was so that we could take only those cases that we were interested in. Okay, so we don't have that many cases, but it doesn't mean I have to work every day. Of course there was a compromise. I had to do the tail of the Durbin idiot for the night. Oh well.

The lead story in the *Portland Press Herald* was the recovery of the painting. Tim, Derek, and I remained unnamed and were referred to as "museum security," which was what we had wanted in order to keep our cover. The story gave the background of the painting. The artist, Maxwell Littlefield, was a local artist who was famous for his landscapes. *The Majorette* was one of his few portraits. It was painted in 1938 and depicted a middle-aged woman dressed up in a blue and red majorette uniform. The model was painted in such a way that she seemed to be staring straight out of the frame. Many people, including myself, found it disturbing. The painting would be reframed and then put back on display. I cut out the article and planned to add it to the agency's files.

I busied myself in the kitchen and placed the ingredients for lasagna in the slow cooker. Dinner would be ready when Tim got home. I took a book and settled down in a comfy chair for the morning. Argus quickly jumped onto my lap and was soon snoring away. I was just getting into the book when I heard a knocking on the door.

"Hey Jesse," called Rhonda from the front door.

"In here," I yelled. Argus was already tearing his way to the front door to greet her.

"I heard you were taking the day off, so I thought I'd stop by," she said as she stepped out onto the porch. Now don't get me wrong. I love my friends, but sometimes I just need to take some alone time to recharge my batteries.

"I heard on the news that someone recovered the stolen painting. It was you guys, wasn't it? That must have been exciting!"

"It was surprising at any rate. Of course, like most things that happen to me, it raises more questions. We have the painting, but we have no idea why it was hidden in the museum or who took it." Rhonda sat down in the rocking chair and Argus quickly jumped up in her lap. I told her the story of our search of the museum and how I happened to stumble onto the hiding place.

"The reason I stopped by," said Rhonda, "is to remind you that All Souls' annual softball game is coming up. You and Tim are two of our best players. And by the way, I haven't seen you in church for a few weeks."

"I'm trying to get my life organized. We'll be at the softball game."

"Good to know."

"So what's up with you?" I asked.

"Jackson keeps asking me to marry him again."

"And?"

"Well, you know, I don't want to ruin a good thing."

"What makes you think that getting married will ruin anything?" I asked.

"Just look at my track record." It was true. She had been married several times and none of them had worked out.

"Two things you need to remember. Jackson, unlike your previous liaisons, is not a loser. And you are also much older and wiser. Let me repeat, much, much older."

"Anyway," she said to change the subject, "Jackson and I are going on a cruise. We are taking a windjammer out of Camden with your friend Parker Reed."

"You must like it. This is your second cruise."

"Love it and the food…"

"You don't have to sell me on it. Remember, I'm the one who encouraged you to go. I spent two great summers cooking on the *Doris Dean*.

"So would you mind checking on the house and watering the plants?"

"Of course not. When are you going?"

"Right after the softball game. In about two weeks."

Having given me the update, Rhonda excused herself and I went back to reading. Argus settled down and was napping under my chair. I had no more than twenty minutes of reading when there was another knock at the door.

"Hello Jesse," came a voice through the screen door. I recognized pastor Mary Bailey's voice.

"Come on in, Mary. I'm out on the back porch." Argus ran to greet her and escorted her back.

"I wanted to ask you something," said Mary as she took the rocking chair that Rhonda had just vacated.

"Ask away," I said. "Rhonda was just here and reminded me about the softball game."

"The deacons came up with the idea of having a bean-hole supper, open to the public, after the softball game. I wanted to run it past you."

110

"I haven't been to one for years," I answered. "It was great community builder in its day."

"I was wondering how much you knew about them?" I was beginning to see where this was going. I always seemed to be the first responder when it came to food issues.

"It's a lot of work," I said, hoping to make it sound difficult. "It takes a lot of people and time to make it work. It takes about two days of preparation. You need to dig a hole in the ground, line the hole with rocks, burn a fire down to the coals, take a large covered vessel, place the beans in the vessel, cover it and bury it for overnight, dig it up, and serve. Usually you need at least two pots for different bean recipes. Then you need ham, hotdogs, brown bread, and so on to serve a meal"

"I knew you would know what to do! Can I count on you to organize it?" she asked sweetly. I didn't like where this was going.

"I'll need at least a group of twenty people and two huge cast iron cauldrons," I answered. I was pretty sure cast iron caldrons would be difficult to find.

"Perfect! Jimmy Jordan has three cast iron covered cauldrons in his antique store. He's going to give them to the church. We can do this every year!"

"That's great," I said gritting my teeth and trying not to. I think Mary set me up for this one!

Mary excused herself and I went back to reading and Argus went back to sleeping. The day was warm and there was a slight breeze, and the book I was reading was really entertaining.

"Hey Jesse, can you come out and play?" I recognized the voice of Billy Simpson.

"Out here on the porch." Argus was already on his way to greet Billy. Somehow my quiet day was not going according to plan.

"I heard you had the day off and I thought I'd take you to lunch."

"Sure," I said. Billy looked healthy and happy after his stint in rehab.

"I haven't seen you much since you and Tim took over the Bigg-Boyce agency. I didn't think there was all that much to do here."

"Neither did I. And we haven't made much progress."

"Are you doing okay? I know what a shock Kelley's death probably was, even though it's been years."

"I'm doing okay. I'm more concerned with her husband, Jim Freeman. He asked me to look into the murder. The police put him in jail, but his lawyer got him released when it was clear that he couldn't have done the second murder."

"Do you think he did it?" asked Billy.

"My gut feeling is that he probably didn't."

"I've known you for a long time, and I'd trust your gut feelings any day."

"Thanks! I need a favor." I went on and told Billy about the bean hole supper. "I need a second in command."

"I'd be happy to help. It would be like old times, our working together. Now let's go to Wong Ho's. I'm buying."

. . . .

112

After a pleasant and relaxing lunch Billy dropped me back at Eagle's Nest. Argus was ready for his afternoon walk, so I took him up the street for exercise, careful not to go too far because it was getting too warm for him to exercise. We returned to the house and I resumed reading. I was lost in the story I was reading when suddenly I heard a familiar voice.

"Have you found Jesus?" yelled Jason Goulet through the front door.

"Yes," I yelled back. "He's hiding in the bathroom." Argus launched himself off my lap and was on his way to greet Jason.

"I thought I'd come over for a beer. I never see you anymore."

"Beer's in the 'fridge."

"I went over to the office to see you, and Jessica said you had the day off and sent me over here."

"Did she?" I'd have to have a talk with her. My reading time was seriously being sacrificed today for social connections. Maybe I needed to spend more time keeping in touch with people. I guess time management was not one of my stronger traits. Jason handed me a beer and sat down.

"What have you been up to?" he asked. I gave him the rundown, omitting the details, but touching the highlights.

"And you haven't really solved anything?"

"Not yet. But I think we're close on a few things." We chatted for a while between sips of beer.

"Look at the time," said Jason. "I need to get home or Monica will be wondering where I am."

Jason left and I resumed my reading. Argus was napping but sat up suddenly with his ears on full alert. I knew from experience that Tim's car had just turned

113

onto the street. Argus recognized the sound of the car and ran to sit by the door. Tim came in and scooped up a squirming Argus.

"How was your quiet day off?" he asked.

"What quiet day off?" I asked. I went on and told him about my many visitors.

"Well aren't you the social butterfly!"

Chapter 17

The night was quiet. It was too late in the season for spring peepers and too early for crickets. The wind direction had changed, and the sea breeze had cooled down the evening. Thankfully there were no insects buzzing around tonight, the wind keeping them at bay. I was sitting in the nondescript Corolla waiting to catch sight of James Durbin's car. I wanted to wrap up this case and send Jayne Durbin on her dizzy way. Sometimes I envy those persons who are not burdened with deep thoughts and common sense!

The reality of a stake out isn't at all what it is on TV. Usually it's hours sitting around waiting for something to happen. After the first hour you become so bored you begin talking to yourself. By the third hour it becomes evident that the cup of coffee you finished earlier wasn't such a good idea.

Finally I saw Durbin's car pull out of the parking lot as his work shift got over. I pulled in behind him as we eased into traffic. Tonight he wasn't heading for his usual haunts, but headed south on the highway. I slowed down and pulled back, but kept an eye on his car. Unlike last time he didn't get off at the Freeport exit, but kept on going. I glanced down at the fuel gauge and was glad to see that the tank was almost full. It would be a real bummer to have to stop and gas up when in pursuit.

Wherever James Durbin was going he seemed to be in no hurry because he was traveling well below the speed limit. I was finding it a challenge to drive that slowly. After about thirty minutes he signaled to turn off the exit to Baxter Boulevard in Portland. I followed at a discrete distance. Durbin turned up several side streets. I was afraid that he had spotted me and was trying to lose me, but after a few more turns he pulled up in front of a neat little white cape style house, got out, and walked up the walk. I drove by slowly and watched as best as I could. The door opened and Durbin stepped in.

It was too dark for me to read the street number on the house, so I parked the car, got out, and sauntered past the house. I had to practically walk up to the front door to read the number, but I jotted it down and headed back to the car.

I picked up the phone and dialed the office. I knew Derek was working on the alarm accounts and probably Jessica would be there to keep him company. Derek answered on the third ring.

"What's up?" asked Derek.

"I want you to check out an address for me and tell me who lives there." I gave him the address.

"No problem. I'll get right on it."

Just then I heard a tapping on my car window. I looked up to see James Durbin staring at me and not looking pleased at all.

"Never mind," I said to Derek and hung up.

....

By my third cup of coffee the next morning I was beginning to feel a little more awake. The second jelly donut didn't hurt either, I might add. It was a good thing because Mrs. Jayne P. Durbin was sitting in a chair opposite my desk. She was wearing a little black dress that was little more than an oversized tube top. Tim was standing behind me as I handed her the report I had just finished typing.

"It's all in the report," I said as she looked at the file. "Your husband was sneaking around, and he was meeting up with another woman. But the other woman was your sister, and they were meeting to plan your fortieth birthday party. Though how you could possibly be forty is a mystery to me." Women, I found, appreciate a compliment even when they suspect that it's complete bullshit.

"Thank you," she said as she whipped out her check book. "If you give me the bill I'll settle up right now."

I handed her the bill and she wrote out a check. We both walked her to the door where she gave us both a hug,

"Case closed!" I said to Tim as I handed him the check.

Tim looked at the check and gave me a thumbs up!

The afternoon was slowly ticking by, and Argus was getting restless and began pacing the office.

"You need to go out?" I asked. Argus jumped up and barked, so I put his harness on and took him for a walk down by the waterfront. After he did his business and I cleaned it up, I sat down on a bench to watch the river.

"Hello, Jesse." I turned around to see Jim Freeman walk up and sit down on the other end of the bench. "Jessica told me you were out walking the dog."

"Jim, I'm glad to see you out of jail!"

"The police let me go. I'm no longer a suspect. I've been demoted to a person of interest

"Do they have any other suspects?" I asked.

"No. Not really. They think the two murders must be related, and of course I was in jail at the time of the second murder."

"That's good news!"

"Yes, but someone killed my wife, and tried to make it look like I did it. I want to ask you to look into her murder."

"I'm sure the police are doing that," I said.

"Yes, but you were married to her once, too. You have a vested interest in the outcome as much as I do. And the police don't have the time or resources to spend. I have some money from her insurance and can pay you."

I sighed. "I'll only charge for expenses. The rest is *gratis*."

"Thanks Jesse. You're a good person."

"Okay, now why don't you tell me the whole story."

"Kelley had been working at the museum for about a year. She really seemed to like it. Her job was to raise funds, write grants, and handle donations. She was good with money and they seemed to like her. About the time the painting was stolen, she said money began to disappear from various accounts. She alerted the auditor and they both went over the accounts, but couldn't find anything unusual that they could pin on anyone."

"And now they're both dead. I'm sure the police don't think the deaths are a coincidence."

"No, they don't, which is why they let me go."

"So Kelley had gone away to do some painting, as far as you knew?"

"Yes, she said she didn't know where exactly she was going, but that if I needed her, I could call her on her cell phone."

"Did you call her?"

"No, she called me the first day to tell me that she arrived safely and would be back in a few days."

"So you talked to her?" I asked.

"No, she called while I was at work and left a message."

"And that's the last you heard from her?"

"Yes, then two days later you guys found her dead at the museum."

"And where were you all this time?"

"I was home. And as I said before, I was just taking it easy."

We shook hands and Argus and I started back up to Front Street and the office.

Chapter 18

The rain began sometime after midnight. The loud clap of thunder woke me. Argus doesn't like thunder and burrowed down under the covers between me and Tim. Tim slept on, oblivious of the storm. I always admire anyone who can sleep through the night undisturbed.

I knew we needed the rain, and I hoped the storm would bring in cooler weather. So far the summer had been hotter than usual, even though it was only June. If June was so hot, what would July be like?

Since I was awake I padded out to the living room and listened to the weather radio. Severe storm warnings were issued for Lincoln and Sagadahoc counties. The next lightening strike made me jump up from the chair. Not only had the lightening startled me, but I thought I saw the outline of a person outside the window. I ran up to the window and looked out, but there was nothing there. My imagination was working overtime. I went back to bed.

After breakfast the next morning I found Tim kneeling on the ground examining the earth under the window.

"It wasn't your imagination," said Tim. "There are tracks here, someone was out here in the rain last night."

"That's not good," I said, stating the obvious. "Can you tell anything by the tracks?"

"Someone with adult size boots, but this isn't television, and unlike a crime show, it's almost impossible to trace shoe prints. There are just too many brands, and many of them share the same tread, plus they are so cheap that anyone can buy a pair of shoes or boots for cash. Unless someone is arrested and we can match the prints, it's impossible to trace."

"You mean television programs make stuff up?" I asked in mock shock.

"I'm afraid they do," answered Tim.

Living with an ex-cop, I never felt the need for a security alarm for Eagle's Nest, but since we had a nocturnal visitor peeking in the windows, I made a note to have an alarm system installed; after all, we owned a security company and half of our business was monitoring alarms.

I was staring at the folder on my desk containing the files of the Turner Art Museum. It reminded me of teaching when I had a pile of research papers on my desk. I would stare at the pile dreading all the work it would take to get through it. I was feeling the same dread, but I picked up the file and started to read through it again, hoping something would pop out at me.

We had debunked the spooky feeling people had in the gallery, the feeling that they were being watched. The electrical energy from unshielded electric cables had been to blame. Most likely active imaginations and susceptible personalities also played a part. We had also found a painting that had been missing for months. Not a bad track record, except for the fact that there had been two murders at the museum. And there was still the mystery of things being moved in the museum with no explanation. I picked up the phone and dialed William Baker at the museum.

"Can you fax me the specs on the security cameras?" I asked.

"Sure. What do you need them for?"

"Just a theory I want to check."

"Okay, I'll get them to you sometime this morning."

"Thanks." I hung up. The hair on the back of my neck was standing up and I knew I was on to something.

I was on my second cup of coffee when I heard the whirring of the fax machine in the outer office.

"That was fast," I said to Jessica as I walked into the main office to retrieve the fax. "It's only been an hour since I asked Bill Baker to fax me over some specs."

I reached for the fax, but realized it wasn't from Bill Baker, but from Helen at the registrar's office at the university. I froze.

"What's wrong?" asked Jessica.

"Nothing; I had forgotten about this. I asked my friend Helen at the university to send me a class list of all the people in Bryan Landry's art class." I looked to the cover sheet. Helen apologized for taking so long to get back to me, but apparently the class list had "disappeared" and she had to do some detective work to find it. Finally she had to contact the instructor and get the list from him.

I flipped to the second page and ran my eyes down the class list.

"Shit!" I said out loud. Two names stood out as I looked down the list. One was Bryan Landry and the second was Kelley Kennedy!

"Time to go home," said Tim from the doorway. I looked at the clock and it was four-thirty already. Argus heard Tim and began jumping around. The fax with all

122

the security specs had arrived by mid-afternoon, and I felt like I had been staring at them for hours.

"Sorry, I've been so focused on these specs I've not planned anything for dinner."

"No problem. I'll stop at Wong Ho's for takeout and meet you back at the house." One thing I loved about Tim was his flexibility.

"Thanks big guy. I owe you."

"I'll collect later," he said and was gone.

....

The morning was warm and sunny with a slight breeze off the ocean. Argus was napping under my desk and enjoying the air that was coming in through the open window of my office. Both Tim and I were convinced that there was some significance to the fact that both Kelley Kennedy and Bryan Landry were in the same art class, but we were unable to figure out what it could be. For the time being I was working on the museum happenings to see what I could figure out. I was staring at the specs of the museum's security system trying to figure out if there was something I wasn't seeing. Pictures don't move themselves, so there had to be some type of explanation.

Each gallery had a camera that did a slow sweep of the room. They were synchronized and each camera followed an exact pattern for each sweep. If anyone had tinkered with a camera an alarm would have sounded. So much for that idea! I closed my eyes and tried to visualize the museum coverage, and then I saw it! If I was right, at least one mystery would be cleared up.

123

Bill Baker, Tim, Derek and I were sitting in the security office watching the security monitors in the galleries.

"What exactly do you think you are going to see?" asked Bill Baker as we watched people milling around in the museum.

"Nothing yet! As soon as the people leave I want to try something," I said.

"The galleries will close in about twenty minutes. Anyone want coffee?" Bill offered. We all said yes and Bill went to get us some.

"You sure this will work?" asked Derek.

"Not really, but it's worth a try," I answered.

....

Everyone had left the museum except for Bill and Tim. During the day the hidden cameras were controlled by a security officer who could move and zoom the cameras and follow the visitors around. At night the cameras were set to automatic and would sweep each gallery in a pre-ordered fashion. If I was right, I could time the camera movements and move about undetected.

From the staircase I waited for the first sweep of the main gallery camera and then headed into the coat room and from there into the men's room. There were no cameras in the restroom area as that was considered by some of the staff to be an invasion of privacy. I took out a stop watch. It would take the cameras exactly two minutes to scan each of the galleries. The field of vision for each camera was very narrow because the security company who set up the cameras thought it more important to focus up close on the works of art, rather than a wide view of the galleries during the night time when no one would be in the museum.

124

I waited two minutes and ten seconds and stepped out into the main gallery. I went to the nearest painting on the wall and lifted it off its wall mountings and placed it carefully on the floor. I walked slowly into the next gallery and waited for the next sweep to begin and stepped into the room and walked close to the wall. I went to the middle of the room, lifted off a glass case and set it on the floor. I picked up a small Remington sculpture and placed it on the floor beside the glass case.

In ten minutes I had gone through the entire museum and moved a piece of art in each of the galleries. If my research and timing were correct, I was virtually invisible to Bill and Tim. I was walking between the camera sweeps.

"Jesus Christ, Jesse," exclaimed Tim when I returned to the security office.

"How did you do that?" asked Bill Baker with a stunned look. I could see on the monitors the havoc I had caused. Tim pushed some buttons on the recorder and played back the videos. I watched the screen carefully. The cameras did a sweep of the galleries and everything looked normal until the second sweep, when the cameras revealed items disturbed in each gallery. There was no sign of human presence.

"The place isn't haunted," I said, "except by the living." I went on to explain how I cracked the timing code of the camera by reading the specification sheets the security company supplied.

"Which also explains," added Tim, "how the Majorette painting was stolen and nothing appeared on the videos.

"At least we got that back," sighed Bill. "That is one of our signature pieces."

"Really?" I asked. To me it looked like a painting of a hooker in a bad Halloween costume. No accounting for taste, I guess. Then I remembered that Kelley was dressed up like the painting when she was murdered. "Give me some background on the painting."

"The painting," began Bill, "is one of the first acquisitions of the museum's trust fund. It was painted in 1938 by Maxwell Littlefield. He was a Maine artist who painted on Monhegan Island in the twenties and thirties. He is usually known for his landscapes. The subject is said to be his wife, who was a former circus entertainer. She drowned in a boating accident in the early forties. Rumor has it that he had her killed, but it was never proven. He died shortly after that and his paintings shot up in value." I knew most of this story. But the fact that the subject was his wife was news to me.

"How much is it worth now?" asked Tim.

"Art is a funny thing. Put up for auction it could go for a small fortune, or it could sell for around a hundred bucks. Depends on who wants it and how badly. We have it insured for around five hundred thousand."

"Did you get the insurance when it went missing?" I asked.

"No, the insurance company was stalling. They said it looked like an inside job."

"Well," said Tim, "I think it was, too!"

Chapter 19

L ate afternoon slipped slowly into evenings as a cooling breeze from the Atlantic swept over the Maine coast. The brilliant red sunset promised another perfect summer day. Most likely there would be fog tomorrow morning, and then the sun would burn off the gloom and reveal a brilliant day of light and shadow.

Five teenagers from the All Souls' youth group gathered around me as I gave instructions. We were assembled in the backyard of the church. A rental company was setting up tents and tables in preparation of the upcoming bean hole bean supper. The preparations were all guess work as we had no idea how many people would attend. We could count on most of the church members to show up as well as the opposing softball team from St. Luke's Episcopal Church. Beyond that it was a crap shoot as to how many others would join us. I enlisted Billy Simpson to help me organize the super. He was glad to have something to do.

"We need three holes," I said, "each about three feet deep. We need rocks to line the holes and wood to build a roaring fire. Mr. Mallory and Mr. Goulet are bringing in several loads of wood, and we have volunteers out scouring the woods looking for rocks. When you start digging, be sure to dust off and put in a pile any rocks you find. We can use as many as we can get." The last ice age had insured that Maine soil would never be short of rocks. It was one reason that New England has miles and miles of stonewalls everywhere.

In the church kitchen, the church ladies were busy parboiling the beans and preparing the side dishes and desserts. Without church ladies, I always said, organized religion would never have happened. Three very large, cast iron covered pots had arrived. They were so heavy that it took two men to move them.

There was a festive air to all the preparations. I seemed to be the only one who was worried about the success of the supper. Everyone else was looking forward to tomorrow's softball game and the bean supper to follow.

Several more youth group members arrived and began stacking wood when Tim and Jason arrived with the load. As was typical of today's teenagers, the girls made a point of sharing the heavy lifting and digging with the boys. In fact, by the time a truckload of rocks arrived, it was an all girl team who unloaded and stacked the rocks.

Pastor Mary Bailey made a point of circulating around to the various working groups to offer thanks and praise. Once the holes were finished the youth volunteers lined the holes with rocks. Two of the church members were firefighters and volunteered to supervise the teenagers as they built roaring fires in the pit. I had Billy Simpson stand around with a fire extinguisher in case anyone was so unwise as to set himself or herself on fire.

I busied myself coating the cast iron kettles with oil, while another group of church members fired up a gas grill to cook up burgers and hot dogs for the workers' lunch. Once the fires were going in the pits, we gathered under one of the two tents for lunch. The festive atmosphere continued. The old adage "many hands make for light work" seemed to apply. We had more than enough workers and no one had too much to do.

After lunch the beans were brought out and poured into the cast iron pots. We mixed in onions, molasses, brown sugar, and other seasonings. There were three types of beans. We had navy beans, great northern, and red kidney beans. One type of beans for each pot.

We waited for hours until the fires died down to hot, glowing coals. The stones in the pit would be extremely hot and would retain heat for hours. We had a team lower each pot into a pit and place the heavy cast iron lids on each one. I covered the lids of the pots with aluminum foil to keep out the sand and grit, and then the kids used shovels and buried the beans.

If all went well, when we uncovered the fire pits tomorrow, we would have some of the best beans in the world. If not, well someone would be making an emergency run to the supermarket to buy up several cases of baked beans.

Once all the side dishes were put away, we all went home and hoped for the best.

. . . .

The bases were loaded and the team was ahead by three runs. Unfortunately it wasn't our team that was ahead. Rhonda was pitching and I was out in left field, hoping I wouldn't have to do anything. I glanced at my watch. If the game went on much longer I would have to sneak out and begin setting up for the bean supper. Reverend Tom from St. Luke's was at bat. St Luke's had two outs and the good reverend already had two strikes. I could see that Rhonda was determined to strike him out. She slowly rolled the ball around in her hands and then quickly threw out a pitch, hoping to catch Tom by surprise.

What happened next happened so quickly that I was caught unaware. Reverend Tom hit the ball and I heard the crack of the bat. I looked up and saw the ball heading directly toward me. Forgetting for a moment that I was a gentleman of a certain age, I leaped up in the air and caught the ball and St Luke's was out. Unhappily, when I touched the ground it was on one foot, and I heard a crunch and felt a shooting pain go through my foot.

I must have yelled out in pain, because suddenly I was surrounded by players and taken off the field, put in an ambulance and taken to the emergency room. "This is hardly serious enough for all this fuss," I complained to Tim. "I need to get to the church and get the supper ready."

"Relax. Billy Simpson can handle the details and you are not irreplaceable."

"No one likes to hear that," I said to Tim. A nurse appeared and wheeled me off to x-ray.

Nothing was broken and I was given a prescription painkiller, told to ice the foot three times a day, and use a cane for a few days.

By the time I got back to the church, the game was over and St. Luke's had won. The pain was starting to recede thanks to the pain killers. A line had formed to buy tickets for the supper and the church ladies had put out the salads, corn bread, and sliced ham. A crowd had gathered around the fire pits as members of the youth group began to dig up the pots. Success or failure hinged on what we would find under the lids. We could have baked beans if we were lucky, or we could have an undercooked mess.

I slowly hobbled over to the crowd on my cane. Billy Simpson had taken charge and I was impressed with his leadership. That was a good thing. Billy had had a hard time of it the last several years and needed something to feel good about.

The crowd made way for me as I hobbled up to get a closer look at the pots. Billy picked up a towel and wrapped it around his hand and lifted off the cover of the first bean pot. A cheer went up from the crowd and I looked into the pot to see a bubbling brown mass of perfectly baked beans.

There were more people at the bean supper than we had anticipated. Fortunately we had more than enough food to feed the hungry crowd. I had been relegated to light duty and sat in a chair with ice on my foot. The beans had turned out perfect, the weather was perfect, the crowd was enthusiastic, and except for the throbbing pain in my foot, I was having a great time.

I got out of my chair and with the help of the cane I made the rounds of the church grounds. I was standing off by myself when I felt a pair of hands grab my ass. I whipped around to find myself looking into the green eyes of Parker Reed.

"How about we go off for a quick one?" said Parker with a smile.

"Tempting," I answered. "But Tim owns a gun, and your boyfriend Billy Simpson is over in the kitchen."

"Ah, well then," replied Parker with a mock sigh of resignation. "What's with the cane? Is it a new fashion statement?"

131

"I sprained my foot trying to catch a softball. It's nothing serious. What are you doing here?"

"I came to spend the weekend with Billy before I have to go off on the next ten day cruise." Parker was the skipper of the windjammer *Doris Dean*. When I first met him back a few years ago he was the first mate and I was filling in for the cook who had jumped ship mid-voyage. We had a memorable summer that year.

"Parker," said Tim with a nod as he stepped out of the crowd. "Here to see Billy?"

"Sure, that's it," answered Parker. It was a typical meeting of two alpha-males. I was beginning to feel uncomfortable. Fortunately Billy Simpson appeared beside Parker.

"Everything is going well. I think we should all grab some food and sit for a while," said Billy.

"That's a great idea!" I answered. We stood in line, got our beans and ham, and found a table under the tent. Rhonda and Jackson, Monica and Jason were already there and had saved us a seat.

"I've never had bean hole beans before," stated Rhonda. "These are excellent!"

"It's the slow cooking that does it. Plus there is very little liquid lost underground. It makes a big difference," I replied. "Thanks for taking over, Billy. You did a great job." And I meant it.

"Thanks, Jesse, but most of the work was already done. How's your leg by the way?"

"Just a little bit of throbbing, but the ice helped. Parker, what's the ten day cruise about. Aren't most of your cruises either four or seven days?"

"There's going to be a tall ships flotilla off the coast of Nova Scotia, and a lot of the windjammers are going. It should be quite an event."

I was about to say something else when my cell phone rang. Only a few people have my number and most of them were sitting here with me. I looked at the caller ID and saw it was Derek. I knew Derek was working.

"Hello Derek, what's up?" I listened to what he was saying on the other end. "I see. Thanks for letting me know." I hung up.

"What's happening?" asked Tim, looking a little concerned.

"That was Derek. He just got a call at the station. Jim Freeman's house has been ransacked!"

Chapter 20

My gun was drawn and my heart was pounding. Danger could pop up anywhere! Out of the corner of my eye I saw movement and aimed my gun with my finger on the trigger. Luckily I hesitated for a moment, because the movement was a child darting out in front of me. I lowered my gun briefly when another danger popped up in front and started toward me. I aimed for the heart and pulled the trigger. The bullet exploded with a power that sent shock waves down my arm.

"Excellent!" said the firing range instructor as he examined the human-shaped paper target. You didn't shoot until you were sure of your target and then you aimed carefully without panic."

"Thanks, but I'm not so sure I'd be as cool in real life."

"None of us is; but practice and skill are helpful."

I emptied the ammo and put the gun away, following all instructions of gun safety. "Thanks," I said to the instructor. "I'll be back for my second lesson."

"Okay, Jesse. Good job on your first lesson."

"Thanks!" I grabbed my cane and got in my car to go over and see Jim Freeman. His house was about two miles away. I had no idea Kelley lived that close to me. I was there in no time. He greeted me at the door.

"What happened to you?" he asked.

"I tried to catch a softball. It's just a sprain. And the cane is rather a nice fashion statement, don't you think?"

"Oh, yes. Quite."

"So tell me about the break-in," I suggested. He led me into his living room. I looked around and it gave me the willies. There were pictures of Jim and Kelley everywhere. There were some, too, of Kelley when she was younger, around the time I was married to her. In fact, one of those pictures I had taken of her on our honeymoon. Yeesh!

"There's not much to tell. I went out shopping on Saturday afternoon. When I came back the back door was open and everything inside was a mess."

"What did they disturb?"

"All the drawers in the house had been pulled out and dumped. All the cushions had been pulled off the sofa and the chairs, and all the closets had been ransacked."

"Was anything missing?"

"No, not that I'm aware of. Of course I really don't know if Kelley had anything in her desk or closet..." At this his eyes welled up with tears. He took a deep breath as if to get hold of his emotions. You've got to find out who did this!"

"I intend to! But right now I'm concerned about you. Any idea who would do this or why?"

"Not at all. Why would someone do this?"
"There are a lot of deranged people around. It could be for any reason, or none at all. I'm just worried that it may be more than just a random break-in. Bath doesn't have a lot of crime and it's got to be more than a coincidence that your wife was murdered and then your house was burglarized."

"You really think so?"

"That's what my gut says," I replied. Actually it was my mostly dormant sixth-sense that was telling me that. Actually the inner voice was more like screaming

135

at me, but sharing that information wasn't going to be helpful.

"What should I do?"

"You should install an alarm system. The Bigg-Boyce agency, as you know, installs and monitors alarm systems. We could set one up for you tomorrow." Might as well give a sales pitch while I'm at it.

"That would be great. Do you have an alarm system?"

"Ah, sure. We use it all the time when we are out." It was partly true. The office was alarmed, and we do use it when we think of it. The house wasn't alarmed. I never saw the need, since I live with an ex cop. "Do you mind if I look around? Maybe you'll notice something missing if you give me the guided tour. Tell me what each room looked like."

"Sure thing, right this way." He led me into the kitchen and described how the drawers were open and the cupboards were emptied out onto the floor. "The cupboards hadn't been cleaned out in a while. I threw most of the stuff out."

"None of the knives were missing?" I asked. It seemed like a question I should ask, but maybe I watched too many crime dramas on TV.

"None were missing, but I did find one in the living room."

"Which on?"

"It was this one." He held up a big butcher knife to show me. I hate knives and to see one being held up in front of me made me more than a little nervous.

"Okay then," I said carefully taking the knife from him and setting it down. I had a sudden vision of the knife being carried by a killer. If Jim had been home, I think he would be dead now. "I think it was a good thing you weren't home. Maybe we can get that alarm system put in today." I pulled out my cell phone and made a call to the office. Jessica picked up and I told her to get someone over here today to install the alarm.

Next Jim took me into the bedroom. Unlike the rest of the house that had nice matching furnishings, this room was furnished with odds and ends. The first of the closets had Jim's clothes. The second was empty.

"I gave away all her clothes to charity after the funeral. I couldn't stand to see them anymore." It was a natural reaction and I understood how that must have felt.

"Had her stuff been disturbed in this room?" I asked.

"Not as much. The closet doors were opened and that was about it."

"Interesting," I mumbled. I had no idea what the significance of that was. As it stood, I really had no idea what I was doing at all.

According to Jim the bathroom hadn't been touched at all, Last of all he took me into the small second bedroom. This was used as Kelley's home office.

"This room was really torn apart, but there isn't a lot of stuff in here" Jim informed me.

Stepping into this room sent chills down my spine. My sixth-sense was yelling at me to pay attention. "What did she use this room for?"

"She kept her projects in here. The sewing machine, the computer, her knitting yarn, books she was reading. She liked having a place where she didn't have to put anything away." Funny, I thought, I don't remember her ever putting anything away! Best not to say that out loud, though.

"Something's wrong here," I blurted out before I could stop myself.

"What is it?"

"Didn't you say that she had a computer?"

"Yes, a top-of-the-line laptop."

"Where is it?" I asked. All I saw was an empty case and an empty spot on her desk. I didn't see anything else around.

"Oh, my god! You're right. I never gave it a thought. It's missing. It was here before. I just never come into this room. She had some notes in her computer case as well, and they're gone!"

"So there is something missing after all?"

"Yes, there is. Do you think this has any meaning?"

"Oh, yes," I answered. "This changes everything!"

I filled Tim in on things when I got back to the office. He listened carefully and then held his hands up to his head like it was going to explode.

"Things just get more complicated whenever you get involved. And now we have to find out who killed Kelley, and," he pointed out, "we are only charging him for expenses."

"We're not working for the money," I reminded him. "We are working for the adventure, otherwise we would be sitting around at Eagle's Nest rocking on the back porch."

"There are days when I'd like to do that."

"We'll have plenty of days to do that, but right now we're on a case. And I think you need some coffee, and maybe a little something else if we can work it into our schedule."

"That might just do the trick," Tim smiled just as Argus jumped up into his lap. "At least we are done with the museum."

"Not quite," I reminded him. "We still have the ghost photos at the museum to debunk."

"Shit, I forgot about that."

"Don't worry, I've got an idea."

....

Until now, all of my recent visits to the Turner Art Museum had been in the guise of security officer. We had been on duty mostly when the museum was closed. I hadn't had a chance to check out the staff during regular museum hours. The very efficient blonde at the admissions desk swiped my membership card and handed me a map of the museum.

"Have the murders here kept people from coming to visit?" I asked. Might as well just jump in feet first!

"Actually," she said, "attendance has been up since the murder."

"I'm sorry," I said. I was on a fishing expedition and I was afraid she might catch on. "It must be difficult coming into a place where your co-workers were killed. Were you close to them?"

"Not really. I work out here mostly, and they were in the offices across the street. I hardly ever saw them except at staff meetings."

"Thanks," I looked at her name tag, "Barbara. Have a great day." She didn't look like a killer, so I continued into the museum.

139

I took out my camera. If I was right, I would be able to reproduce the ghost photos without any problems. When you enter the museum, there is a small gallery containing glass and pottery displays. The main gallery is separated from the glass and pottery exhibit by huge doors of glass. Most of the photographs in question were taken in the main gallery. I waited until a group of visitors stepped into the gallery behind me. I picked up my camera and aimed it through the glass doors into the main gallery.

I looked at the digital display screen on the back of my camera. Sure enough there was a picture of the gallery and several ghostly images seeming to float in the middle of the gallery. The camera had captured the reflection on the glass of the people behind me. Mystery solved!

As long as I was there, I thought I should have a look around. The stolen painting had been reframed and returned to its place in the gallery. I wanted to take a look.

The Majorette was a rather large painting done in garish blue and reds. Beside it was a new display sign the read "Stolen Painting." It explained that the painting disappeared and was found hidden in an air shaft in the museum by a "security officer." No mention of me by name. Oh, well!

I looked at the painting and then the warning light went off in my head. I hate when that happens! There was something I was supposed to see that I just wasn't seeing. "Okay Grandma," I said out load, "you better help me with this one." I wasn't convinced that Dead Granma could hear me, but I'd take any help I could get at this point.

Just before I left the museum, I went into the gift shop and bought a book detailing the Turner's art collection. I figured it would be helpful to study up on the "The Majorette."

Chapter 21

June had been an unpredictable month so far this year. There were days of rain followed by days of hot, humid sun. While the local vegetation was thriving, most of the human population was suffering from allergies. Lilacs had passed and now pink and purple lupines were in bloom and the air smelled sweet and fresh after last night's rain. Tim and I were having our morning coffee on the back porch. Argus was watching the squirrels frolic in the backyard. It was the first day of summer and it was going to be a good day.

"We've wrapped up the case at the museum," said Tim between sips of coffee.

"Except for the murder part," I reminded him.

"Yes, except for that. But we've wrapped up the case as far as Bill Baker is concerned. We've proved that the museum is not haunted and that's what we were paid to do."

"Call Bill Baker and tell him that we have almost finished the investigation and will have a report for him at the end of next week. I still want some time to snoop around the museum. Something just doesn't feel right."

"When you say something doesn't feel right you mean..." he hesitated.

"Exactly," I said. Tim knew that my intuition was pretty accurate, and sometimes downright scary.

Derek and Jessica were already at the office when we arrived. Argus made a beeline straight for Jessica, and then ran over to greet Derek.

"The Freeman alarm is installed and working. I did the installation myself. He also told you

142

discovered that a laptop computer and some notes belonging to deceased were missing."

"Derek, you sound just like a cop. And you know what they're like," I said and gave Tim a look. Jessica just rolled her eyes at me.

"We're taking you out to lunch today," said Jessica. I was just about to say something, but Jessica gave me a look. "Why do you think someone broke into a house to steal a dead person's computer?" she asked, as if to change the subject.

"It's beginning to look a little odd," I said. "First of all a security officer goes missing, then a painting gets stolen from the museum. A woman is found dead on the museum's loading dock dressed up as the subject of said missing painting. Then I learn that Kelley and the missing security officer were in the same art class. Then an auditor turns up dead on the loading dock. And finally someone breaks into the dead woman's house and steals a laptop computer and some notes. Even an idiot can see the puzzle pieces. But none of the pieces fits together yet."

"Or," said Derek, "this could all be an interesting coincidence."

"There's something you need to know about Jesse," said Jessica, "he has a knack about things. He's usually right when it comes to his gut."

I dropped Argus off at the house while we went to lunch. Restaurants don't allow dogs, which is a pity since most dogs are better behaved than some children, and they are certainly less annoying. Fortunately, there were no kids present as school was still in session, thanks to a bad winter and the fact that the kids had to make up the storm days. Derek and Jessica took us to

Ruby's on the water front and insisted that we all have steamed lobster. The waiter gave us all plastic bibs to wear. I usually don't wear them, but since I had to go back to work I put one on. I thought we all looked ridiculous, but I guess it was better than having melted butter on our clothes. I had a good idea why Derek and Jessica were taking us to dinner. I didn't have to wait long to find out.

"We're getting married in two weeks!" said Jessica.

Tim was in the middle of buttering a dinner roll when the knife slipped out of his hand and hit the floor. "What do you mean in two weeks?" blurted out Tim. The waiter slipped away and brought Tim a clean knife.

"It's going to be very informal" broke in Derek. "No invitations, just a few people and that's it."

"You're not thinking of eloping are you?" I asked.

"Oh, no," answered Jessica. "We want you both to be there."

"What about your mother?" asked Tim. "She always talked about having a fancy wedding for you."

"It's not her wedding, it's mine. She's already had two weddings of her own. I'll send her a wedding announcement after the fact. We'll visit her in Florida at Christmas. That should be enough."

"But there must be a lot to do," said Tim. He didn't seem to be taking this well.

"Jesse will help me set it up," Jessica replied and gave me a pleading look. "All you need to do is show up."

Fortunately the red, steaming lobsters arrived; we took the nut crackers and began cracking the shells and dipping the meat into melted butter. I only have lobster a few times a year, but it's always a real treat. I was glad I wore the bib because there was juice and butter everywhere.

The bowl in the center of the table was filling up with discarded shells. I have to admit that eating lobster looks barbaric and primitive. It's always better to eat lobster outside, where you have more room and making a mess isn't so important. That gave me an idea.

"Hey Tim," I said. "Let's have a lobster bake for a Fourth of July cook out. Maybe we can spring Old Lady Lafond from the nursing home. The fourth is her birthday."

"How old is she?" asked Jessica.

"She never says, but she is the oldest living alumna of Morse High. She's the only surviving member of the class of 1930." Tim informed us.

"We could have it in the backyard. I've been meaning to have a gazebo built as a center piece for the yard. Actually, there's a place out on route one that has them premade. All they would have to do is move it and install it. Hey, that might be the perfect setting for an informal wedding." I was talking too fast, but I was trying to distract Tim. It didn't work.

"Dessert anyone?" asked the waiter as he cleared away the empty lobster shells.

We all shook our heads no. When the bill arrived Derek grabbed the check.

"Let me help with this," I offered.

"Oh, no," said Jessica. "It's our treat."

The others left for the office, and I went to Eagle's Nest to pick up Argus. As I turned the car onto to Sagamore Street, I had the uneasy feeling that something was wrong. When I pulled into the driveway, I could see that the front door was open. I knew I had locked it on my way out. As I stepped into the living room, my fears were confirmed. Things had been moved, drawers had been emptied, and my laptop was gone, but they hadn't bothered to take my thumb drive! Fortunately, they hadn't stolen my back-up disk either. All my documents were safe!

In another minute panic set in. Where was Argus?

"Argus!" I yelled going from room to room. I called up Tim and tried to keep the hysteria out of my voice. I ran into the backyard and called for Argus, but no dog anywhere. I entered the kitchen trying to fight back the tears when I heard a scratching sound. "Argus!" I called. More scratching sounds! It was coming from the hall closet. I opened the door and Argus jumped out at me, I picked him up and he started to lick my face.

Tim arrived and Argus ran and jumped into his arms and began licking his face. "I'm glad to see you little guy. Where did you find him?"

"He was locked in the hall closet."

"I'm calling Derek to get over here and install an alarm."

"Good idea," I said as I collapsed onto a nearby chair.

"Someone is going to pay for this!" growled Tim. "Now it's personal!"

Derek arrived in the late afternoon with tools and alarm equipment. I had never had any reason to think that I would need an alarm system for Eagle's Nest. I usually thought that they were installed more to give peace of mind than to deter break-ins. But since we owned a security company, it would be smart to actually use the product. I was certain there would be a lot of false alarms before I got used to it.

I took Argus back to the office with me. There was no way I was letting him out of my sight for a while. Tim had arrived ahead of me and was talking to our insurance agent on the phone, filing a claim for my laptop. Since Jackson Bennett owned the company, I didn't think there would be an issue with the claim.

"What information do have on your laptop anyway?" asked Tim.

"I have some photographs and recipes, plus my cookbook notes. Luckily I keep several backups. The weird thing is there is nothing on there that anyone would want."

"They wouldn't know that. They probably assume that it's your work computer, or that you keep work files on there."

"You think someone wants to get into our work files?"

"Mostly likely, yes."

I surfed the web for the American Shed Company and found the gazebo that would fit perfectly in the backyard. It would be a great addition to the Fourth of July cookout. In fact I had an idea that I would have to talk over with Jessica.

I called the company and was told that they had the gazebo in stock, all they needed to do was deliver it and place it on cement blocks and make sure it was level. They promised to set it up early next week, so I read them my credit card number and they promised to send me a receipt via email.

I went to check my email and sure enough there was a receipt from the American Shed Company. There was also an email from an address that I didn't recognize:

clydea

Hi son,

I bet you never thought your old man would enter the computer age and be using the email. The condo set us all up with the latest, up-to-date service. Your mother refuses to use it, but I say why not!!! Now I can get the latest news all the time. Did you know that the President was a Muslim? I never knew that, but if it's on the web, it must be true. I wish we had Ronald Regan back, now that was a president!

I've been buying up gold, just like the ad on TV says. I read on the web that the global monetary system will collapse and only gold will be valuable. Your mother thinks I'm nuts, but I think she may have a touch of senility.

Anyway, now we can talk on the email all the time,

Your loving father,

Clyde Ashworth.

Oh good grief! My father on the internet, could the day get any worse?

Chapter 22

T he morning was foggy as we drove along the coast. Route one snaked along the coast and in high areas away from the sea it was sunny. The tourist traffic was absent, but we hit pockets of heavy traffic from people going to work. We had plenty of time. Rhonda and Jackson weren't due on the *Doris Dean* until afternoon.

Rhonda was riding shotgun with Argus in her lap. Jackson was in the backseat on the driver's side so Rhonda was able to talk to both of us. I was able to tune her out on the pretext that I was concentrating on driving. Jackson wasn't so lucky.

"And you just wait and see," she said out of the blue. "We'll be the oldest one's on the cruise." Today she was dressed in only what I could describe as a Miss Marple outfit. There's one old bitty that I wouldn't want to be on a cruise with. The Marple woman turned up more dead bodies than a graveyard after an earthquake!

"Not likely," I said. "And even if you are, so what? This isn't your first cruise, you went on the *Doris Dean* two years ago.

"Yes, and last time it was all retired school teachers, and you know what they are like!"

"Two-thirds of this car is populated with retired teachers," I reminded her.

"Yes, but after we retired, we got a life."

Shortly after that remark I pulled the car into the parking lot of Moody's Diner in Waldoboro. It seemed as though there were about fifty other cars there, but we were able to find a small booth to squeeze in.

149

"I don't know when their slow time is, but I've never been here when it wasn't crowded." The place had been in continual operation from the 1930's, and as far as I could tell, it hadn't changed much. But I guess that was the charm.

The waitress brought us coffee and we ordered an early lunch.

"Thanks for house sitting," said Jackson. "I worry about leaving the house vacant, considering that your house got broken into."

"I could sell you a state-of-the-art alarm system."

"Actually that's not a bad idea. We'll talk about it when we return. Insurance companies offer a discount for homes that have a fire alarm component."

"I thought it was overkill, but I'm a believer now," I replied.

"Where's Argus?" asked Rhonda. "You didn't leave him in the car did you?"

"Of course not. He's in the tote bag under your feet." Rhonda looked down and opened the tote bag. Then she noticed the large screened openings on the bag that appeared to be decorations. Argus was curled up in a ball, but awake and listening to us talk."

"How did you get him to do that?" she asked.

"He's pretty smart. He knows that if he's quiet, he gets to go places."

We quickly changed the subject when the waitress returned. "Here are you breakfasts. Anything else you need?"

"No thanks," I said. "I think we're all set."

She reached into her apron pocket and pulled out a dog biscuit. "This is for the dog."

"Busted!" said Jackson.

"How did you know?" I asked.

"I've got the same bag for my dog. Don't forget to tip!" she said with a smile and walked off.

....

I dropped off Jackson and Rhonda with their bags at the head of Camden Harbor and drove off to find a parking spot, which wasn't that easy since it was tourist season and parking was limited. Fortunately I knew the area quite well and was able to secure a spot on a side street near the harbor. I caught up with the two of them by the waterfront near the *Doris Dean* where they were sitting on a bench. The crew members were loading up the ship with food and provisions for the ten day trip.

"You're going to be part of the tall ships flotilla off the coast of Nova Scotia, that should be fun," I said. Seeing the ship there made me somewhat envious.

"Yes, we were lucky to snag the last cabin on the trip," replied Jackson. "I think it helped that we were repeat passengers."

"Not to mention," added Rhonda, "that one of our best friends used to do the nasty with the captain."

"You're a malicious old woman," I replied.

Just then the provisions were stowed away and Parker Reed caught sight of us and waved us aboard.

"Welcome aboard!" said Parker as he reached out his hand to help us climb over the wooden steps. I passed Argus up to him and Parker set him down on the deck. The dog began exploring the ship. "The rest of the passengers will be coming aboard soon. You two are in cabin B in the aft, if you want to go and unpack."

151

"I think I'll go check out the galley and meet you back here in a few" I said and headed toward the bow of the ship and down the steps to the galley.

A young woman in jeans and a tee shirt was in the galley checking out the provisions from a written list.

"Hi, I'm Jesse Ashworth, a friend of Parker's, and I used to be a cook here for a couple of summers."

"Pleased to meet you. I'm Cindy Bishop. This is my first summer cooking for the ship. I love it!" she said. "I've seen your name on several of the recipes." Each cook kept a log with a list of menus and recipes. It was helpful and a great resource that each of us passed along to the next cook.

"I learned more about cooking here than I ever did anywhere else in my whole life."

"Me too! I was really intimidated by the wood stove at first, but I love cooking on it."

"I know," I agreed, "if you can cook on a wood stove, you can cook anywhere.

"There you are," said Parker as he appeared in the doorway, "bothering my cook, no doubt."

"We're having a secret Tupperware party," answered Cindy.

"I should get going," I said. "It was nice to meet you, Cindy. And Parker, it's always interesting seeing you." I picked up Argus, who was ready to go home.

I said good-bye to Rhonda and Jackson, assured them that I would be watching their house, got in my car and headed home.

. . . .

The sun was already up even though it was only six in the morning. I like to think of myself as a morning person, but all that really means is that I wake up early. After my first cup of coffee I can become civil, and after my second cup I become almost human.

I was sitting on the sofa with Argus and sipping my second cup of coffee. Tim and Jessica were busy packing Tim's SUV with camping equipment. Each year the two of them headed off to the wilds of Maine on a camping trip. I was always invited and I always declined. Give up a soft mattress for the hard ground? I don't think so! I knew this year was different, since Jessica would be married soon and probably camping trips with her old man wouldn't be at the top of her To-Do list. At any rate they were both chattering away on what fun it would be sleeping out in a tent under the stars. I suppressed an urge to gag.

"Are you going to be okay by yourself?" asked Jessica.

"I'll be fine," I replied. "I won't be the one shivering in my sleeping bag. Besides I won't be alone, I've got Argus with me." Argus became alert at the sound of his name.

"Use the alarm system," instructed Tim, "so that we don't have to worry about you."

"Are you two going or are you just sticking around to annoy me?" The coffee wasn't working very well. This was going to be a three cup day.

Finally they drove away and I was on my own for a few days. I dressed for the office and tried on my new shoulder holster for my gun. I had my second lesson planned for this morning before I went to the office. Blue shirt, red tie, and I added my dark frame glasses. In the mirror I looked like a professional hit man.

"Your dad is one cool dude," I said to Argus. I harnessed up the dog, punched in the alarm code and headed in to work.

The office was nice and cool when I walked in. Monica was sitting at the desk, taking the place of the vacationing Jessica.

"Good morning cuz," she greeted me. "The coffee is on in the break room. Did you get the Mallorys off safely?"

"As safe as anyone could be, camping out there on the cold ground."

"Jason and I were thinking of going camping sometime."

"I went camping once," I boasted.

"You stayed in a one star motel once!" she replied.

"Exactly my point! That was as close to camping as I ever want to get!" She left the room and returned with two cups of coffee. "Remember when you used to bake muffins in the morning?"

"Yes, back when I was retired. Now I seem to be busy and disorganized. Would you mind looking after Argus while I go for my shooting practice?"

"Not at all. There doesn't seem to be much to do here this morning."

"I know, and we haven't even completed those cases we have. Luckily the alarm installation business is doing okay."

"Have you ever thought of taking over the monitoring of the alarms? Right now the agency installs the alarms for the local people and then you hand over the daily monitoring to an outside company. Why not keep the income for yourselves?"

"Actually," I said, "that's probably not a bad idea! I'll discuss it with Tim, if he makes it back from the jungle."

"Baxter State Park is hardly the jungle."

"Ever been there?"

"Nope."

"Me neither."

....

The smell of gun powder was in the air and the florescent light in the ceiling was flickering. So far I had managed to hit the target several times and only missed once.

"For a beginner," said my instructor, "you have a natural eye."

"I don't expect to ever actually have to use the gun."

"Hopefully not," she replied. "But it's nice to know that you can shoot if you need to. Most people buy a gun and never take lessons. That's a very dangerous thing to do."

I shot at a few more targets, but then my arm was getting tired and my eyesight was getting blurry, and I called it a day.

I got in the car and drove away. There was nothing waiting for me at the office, so I drove by Jackson and Rhonda's house to check it out. I stepped onto the porch to check the mailbox. There wasn't any mail, so I figured they had the post office hold the mail. I took the key and unlocked the door. It had only been a few days, but the house had that shut up smell that houses seem to get when no one is living in them.

155

I checked the plants in the living room, but the soil was damp and they didn't need any water. I was walking toward the dining room when I thought I heard a noise in the kitchen. I stopped in my tracks. My heart was pounding and I drew my gun out of the holster and waited. I heard the sound again. There was no doubt that there was someone in the kitchen. I crept up to the kitchen door, kicked it open and yelled, "Freeze scumbag!"

There was a high pitched scream and there in the middle of the kitchen was Viola Vickner sorting through the mail.

"Don't shoot, Jesse!"

"Viola, what are you doing here?" I lowered my gun and put it back in the holster.

"Rhonda asked me to drop off any mail from the shop that was important. What are you doing here?

"Rhonda asked me to check on the house and the plants. I guess she didn't bother to let us know that we would both be checking."

"I guess not. I think she'll have to be punished for that oversight."

"Got a plan?" I asked.

"Oh, yes. Are you in?"

"I'm in!"

As we were leaving the house she told me of her plan.

"Perfect!" I said when she had finished.

Chapter 23

A big tractor-trailer rig lumbered up Sagamore Street and stopped in front of my house. On the back of the flatbed trailer was a yellow gazebo with white trim. I had it painted to match the house. I wasn't sure how they were going to get it into the backyard, but that was their problem. A crew of workmen pulled up in an extended cab pick-up and started to put in a cement block foundation.

I had roped off the area where I wanted the gazebo placed. I checked in with the guy in charge and put the harness and leash on Argus, packed a bag of freshly baked banana muffins, and headed off to work. I can't stand to be around when my place is being worked on. Not to worry, there was plenty to do in the office.

"You shamed me into getting back into the baking business," I said to Monica as I placed the bag of muffins on the desk. Argus ran over to greet her. She reached down and scratched him on the head.

"These smell great!" she said as she opened the bag and took out a muffin. "This is my last day filling in. Jessica will be back tomorrow. I kind of like working."

"You've been a big help and it's been great having you around. Anything on the work calendar this morning?" I asked.

"Not so far. Business has been slow here from what I've seen."

"Let's go into the break room with our coffee. I need to run some things by you." We took our muffins and coffee to the table. I opened the window and a warm breeze came into the room. The weather was predicted to be perfect for the next few days, but somewhere to the west of us, a heat wave was threatening to invade the east coast.

"What's up?" asked Monica. I was pretty sure she already knew what I wanted to talk about.

"I need a fresh set of eyes on these cases. My subconscious keeps nagging at me about these cases. Somehow I feel that there is a missing link between the painting, the murders, and the missing Bryan Landry. I get a second of insight and then it's gone. It's all very frustrating."

"We were given our intuition for a reason. It's a gift. We were fortunate enough to have a family that supported our spiritual development. Most kids are told that it's all imagination and never get a chance to explore that part of life."

"I suppose," I agreed reluctantly. "It's just never been that reliable. And I'm not totally convinced that it's real at all."

"Doubt is what keeps us grounded. Doubt keeps us from being complete nut jobs. However, too much doubt is just as bad as too much belief. Keep a balanced and an open mind."

"I love talking to you!" I said. "You always make sense."

"I'm pretty certain you already know who killed Kelley Kennedy and Janet Costa."

"Yes, I think I do," I answered. For the first time the vision that was forming in my head came together. "But, I'm missing a few important pieces, like the how and why, not to mention the lack of any physical proof."

"At least," stated Monica as she took the last piece of her muffin and bent down to give it to Argus, "you now have a direction to go in."

The street below me was busy and colorful. There were blooming flowers in planters and colorful awnings on the store fronts. Tourist season was in full swing and Bath was once again vibrant and alive. I stepped back from the window. I knew what I had to do next. If I was correct, everything would fall in place, our outstanding cases would be solved, and a murderer would be brought to justice.

On the other hand, if I was wrong, I'd look like a complete idiot and might hurt some innocent people. There wasn't a lot I could do until Tim and Jessica returned. I'd have to do some foot work, and I couldn't leave Argus alone.

The painting kept bothering me. It was an ugly painting, but somehow it was connected to Kelley's murder. Why was she dressed up like the majorette in the painting? It was one of the most bizarre aspects of the case. Why was the painting hidden in an air shaft? And who the hell would want the painting? I decided to learn all I could about the painting.

The book I bought at the Turner's museum shop was on my bookcase. It contained information and reproductions of the various works in the museum. I picked it up and began thumbing through it. Argus jumped up onto my lap. Whenever I picked up a book he took that as a signal for lap time.

I found the write up for *The Majorette*. There was a lot of information about the artist's life, and a comment on the painting itself, but not a lot of information about his motivation for this particular painting.

I knew the artist was a well-known figure in the 1930's and that I knew I would information about

159

Maxwell Littlefield on line. I went over to my computer and noticed I had a new email:

> From: Bonneya
> Dear son,
> Your father is using the web and he thinks he is now a computer genius. I had to learn to use email, just to keep him in line. Unfortunately he believes everything he reads on the web. I told him you can't trust computers! It's not like television, which you can trust completely. Actually I think your father is going senile. I'll have to keep an eye on him. I hope the agency is doing well. It's about time you got a real job!
> Bonney (your mother)

I sighed; both my parents on the internet. I'd have to start looking for a nursing home, preferably one with a dementia ward! I typed out a brief reply and started to look for information on the painter.

The artist, Maxwell Littlefield, was well-known as a painter of the Great Depression. His works had a garish flare that reflected the misery of the times. Each of his works, said the on-line article, contains an Easter egg. I looked at the several examples and didn't see an egg in any of the photos. It wasn't until I finished the article and looked at the footnotes, that I discovered what an Easter egg was!

I looked back at the picture of *The Majorette* in the book and clearly saw the Easter egg this time.

Funny, I was just in the museum and didn't notice it in the painting. I'd have to go back and check again.

....

"They should be here soon," said Derek as he glanced out the kitchen window. He was helping me get dinner ready. Lately he had been in the kitchen with me helping out whenever he got the chance. At the moment he was lining a pie plate with biscuit dough.

"What's with this sudden interest in cooking?" I asked.

"It's relaxing and you always make it look easy. After a hard day of police work, it's nice to do something fun. I also want to be able to help Jessica around the house when we're married."

I was about to respond when we heard the horn on Tim's Subaru. Tim and Jessica waved at us and then unloaded the camping gear and put it away in the garage.

"What's for dinner?" Jessica asked Derek after she kissed him.

"Hamburger pie and minted peas," answered Derek.

"And rhubarb pie for dessert," I answered after Tim released me from a big bear hug.

"How was camping?" I asked.

"Great weather and we saw lots of wildlife," answered Jessica.

"We had some great father and daughter talks by the campfire," said Tim.

"What did you talk about?" asked Derek.

"Mostly the men in our lives," answered Tim as he winked at me.

161

Derek and I finished getting dinner ready, Tim made the drinks and Jessica served them. We sat down at the kitchen table and began making wedding plans and planning the Fourth of July clambake for the backyard.

"Are you sure?" asked Tim as he stared at the painting. We were at the Turner Museum one last time to finish up our investigation.

"Oh yes, I'm sure." I had just announced to the director, William Baker, and the head curator, Joyce Boyle, that *The Majorette* was a fake.

"But how do you know?" asked Tim.

"Do you know what an Easter egg is?"

"You mean as in the Easter Bunny?"

"An Easter egg," answered Joyce Boyle, "is a hidden message or symbol in a work of art. For instance, Michelangelo painted an image of himself in the Sistine chapel."

"I'm not following," said Bill Baker.

"See that last button on the majorette's uniform?" I asked. "Littlefield always painted a hidden image of himself in his paintings. In the original painting, which is reproduced in the book of the Turner's collection, the last button shows the artist's reflection as he was painting. That's the Easter egg in this painting."

"But I don't see it," observed Tim.

"That's how we know it's a fake." I watched Joyce Boyle visibly turn pale when she realized what I was saying.

"Oh my god! I never noticed that. I just assumed that it had to be the stolen painting," replied Joyce, losing even more color.

"But what does this mean?" asked Bill Baker looking confused.

"It means that *The Majorette* was really stolen and that someone planted a very good forgery for us to find."

"We need to report this to the police at once," said Joyce close to tears.

"We should hold off a day or two," relied Bill Baker. We all looked at him. "We need to think how the publicity will affect the museum. We have an obligation to our board of directors."

"You have an obligation," countered Tim, "to report a major crime."

"And to be honest to the museum members and the public," I added.

"Okay, I'll go call the police now." Bill looked defeated.

....

Tim and I were sitting at a table at Demillo's restaurant in Portland's Old Port section. The restaurant was created from an old car ferry and was billed as a "floating" restaurant. I could feel the very subtle movement of the waves as the tide came in.

"You know something, don't you?" asked Tim. "You've got that look about you."

"What look?" I asked.

"That scary Houdini look you get when you are on to something."

"Houdini look?" Just then the waiter came to take our order. After he scribbled our order and retreated, I continued.

"There's more going on here that we ever imagined. Somehow everything ties into the Turner

Museum. And I have a gut feeling that the key to all this is Bryan Landry. We need to find him and bring him back."

"Explain!"

"Here is what we have so far," I began. "We have a stolen painting, two murders and a missing security guard. Kelley and Bryan were in an art class together. Kelley was murdered and Bryan is in hiding. When I went to find him, he left a note asking if I was trying to get him killed. Then we find the missing painting, only to find out later that it's really a forgery."

"What about the other murder victim? She was an outside auditor. She really didn't work for the museum and didn't know any of the other people."

"I know," I answered. "That part doesn't fit. At least not yet.

"How are we going to find Bryan Landry?" asked Tim.

"I have a plan," I answered.

"I'm sure you do," said Tim with a sigh.

Chapter 24

The sunrise was brilliant red and promised to be a perfect late June Day. My backyard was alive with flowers and birds. Argus was sitting beside me on the floor of the back porch watching the birds fly back and forth to the bird feeder. I was finishing my morning coffee and talking to Connie Thurston on the phone.

Connie was a certified Maine Guide and had just agreed to help me look for Bryan Landry. On March 19, 1897, the Maine legislature required all hunting and fishing guides to register with the state. In the first year there were 1316 guides registered. The honor of being the first registered guide in the state of Maine went to Cornelia Crosby, who was known by the nickname "Fly Rod."

Over one hundred years later Maine Guides continue to promote the love of the outdoors by providing a safe and enjoyable outdoor experience for the many men and women who head out into the Maine wilderness.

Each Maine Guide is also trained to rescue those who become lost in the vast North Country. I was confident that Connie could help me find Bryan Landry, even if he didn't want to be found.

"Are you sure you want to go off by yourself?" asked Tim who had come out to the porch just as I hung up the phone .

"One of us needs to stay behind and take care of business, and Argus needs to be taken care of." Argus looked up when he heard his name. "And, don't forget that you have to start preparing for the Fourth of

July Clam Bake, birthday celebration, and wedding in the back yard.

"Don't remind me! And you be careful out there!" Tim warned. "You know how you are."

"What do you mean by that?" I asked, though I knew exactly what he was saying.

"You think you can handle everything by yourself and you take chances."

"I'll be extremely careful," I answered. I just hoped he didn't see my crossed fingers.

....

By now I pretty much knew my way to Beaver Lake and didn't have to use either my map or my GPS, though I kept the GPS on just to check my progress and arrival time, and okay, the fake human voice was good for company, too.

It was a long trip and I stopped every hour or two to stretch. I was enjoying the ride. The weather was perfect and the gentle green of the summer was broken up by wildflowers all along the side of the road.

I stopped in Bangor for lunch and arrived at the Beaver Lake Inn just before dinner. This trip I was staying in a room in the main lodge instead of one of the cabins. After I unpacked I headed to the kitchen to see Martha Rankin. I was immediately hit with the smell of delicious home cooked food.

"Hi Jesse! It's good to see you. I got your email.

"Good to see you too, Martha. How's John?"

"This is a busy time of year for us. The summer people are returning and John is out straight fixing up the lake cabins and getting them ready for the summer."

"And it must be busy here, too."

166

"About as busy as it can get. The only busier time of year is the fall when it's hunting season."

"Have you heard anything about Bryan?" I asked.

"John thought he saw him out on the lake the other day, but it's hard to tell."

"He must be running out of money by now. He may be ready to come home."

"Connie knows this area like her own back yard. If anyone can find him, she can."

"How well do you know her?"

"She's worked in this area for years. Lots of the sports who stay here use her. You'll like her."

"I should let you get back to work. It smells wonderful in here, by the way."

The dining room was crowded when I arrived for dinner. All the couples were seated at tables for two, the larger groups were seated at bigger tables, and those of us here by ourselves were seated at the largest table in the dining room. There were six of us at the table. I ordered the broiled Atlantic salmon. We were a diverse group and I was the only native Mainer. One guy was here from California to do photography and one of the women was here from Ohio to go bird watching. The remaining three men were all from Philadelphia and planning to get up early and go fishing.

It was fun talking to the other guests, but it had been a long day and after a dessert of molasses pie, I excused myself and headed to my room.

The early morning was chilly and there was dew on the ground. I knew I'd need a jacket and boots for the morning, but I also knew that by late morning the day

167

would most likely become hot once the sun burned off the morning mist.

I had a breakfast of hash and eggs and toast made from homemade bread. It was a heavier meal than I was used to, but I thought it wise to fortify myself for the search.

I was sitting in the lobby having my second cup of coffee when a tall, middle-aged woman walked into the lodge and came up to me.

"You must be Jesse," she said and offered me her hand.

"Nice to meet you Connie. Have a seat. There's coffee over there in the corner if you'd like some."

"I think I will." She walked over, poured out some coffee and sat down beside me. "You gave me some of the information over the phone, and you mentioned that you found his camp site a few weeks ago. The more details I have, the better I can help."

I gave her a detailed account of my last trip to Beaver Lake, including the abandoned campsite and the letter. She asked me a series of questions and took down some notes.

"So you think he must be running out of money?" Connie asked.

"I would think so; it's been a long time."

"We need to find him before he slips over the border and disappears into Canada."

"Wouldn't it be hard for him to get a job with no documentation?" I asked. She just looked at me like I was a passenger on the short bus. "Okay, I suppose it's easy to get fake documents in any country."

"Not to mention fishing boats and lumber camps aren't always concerned with the niceties of documentation," she added.

168

"Where do we start?"

"Let's start where you left off at the old North Land Lumber Camp."

Connie's Jeep was better equipped than my car to navigate the old lumber roads. We were able to penetrate the north woods more deeply and ended up having a shorter hike.

"Do you think he would still be here?" I asked. I was dubious about his returning to the lumber camp.

"Yes, I do! He knew you had left the area. Very few people come this way, and though he has a tent, the abandoned buildings give better shelter in the heavy rain. There is also abundant fire wood here."

We ambled up the road and passed the old railroad engine. The first time I saw it, it gave me the creeps. The huge engine looks so out of place all covered with vines and slightly hidden in the growth. I wouldn't be surprised to see ghostly apparitions hovering around it at midnight. However, I had no intention of finding out.

Connie was carefully looking at the ground as we walked up the road. I looked down to try and see what she was looking at, but I didn't see anything.

"What are you looking at?" I asked.

"Someone was has been up this road recently."

"You can tell that from looking at the ground?"

"Yes, I can. Look closely. It rained two nights ago, which means the gravel on the road shifted during the heavier downpours. If you look carefully, you can see that some of the heavier gravel pieces have been pushed into the softer road. Use a little imagination and you can almost see boot prints."

"I never would have noticed that!" I exclaimed. Had she not shown me what to look for, I never would have believed it. "But it doesn't mean that these are Bryan's footprints."

"No, it doesn't. But it does give us something to begin with."

I stopped to tie my boots, and Connie passed me a bottle of water and an apple. "Time for a break," she added. I sat down on a dry patch of pine needles and Connie consulted her compass. I've never been able to use a compass. All I know is that it supposedly always points north. I took out my GPS and looked at the map on the screen and felt better.

"Don't you use a GPS?" I asked.

"Of course, but it doesn't always work!"

"What do you mean?"

"Take your GPS and stand over there under those trees."

I did as I was told, not sure what she was trying to prove. Then I watched the arrow on the map go from green to yellow. The GPS signal was lost. Then I noticed that the battery was low.

"Okay, I get it now."

"I thought you would."

It was time to continue up the road, and in no time at all we were at the abandoned lumber camp. We searched the several buildings that were still standing. We did find some trash inside, but there was no way to tell if any of it belonged to Bryan or not.

The buildings sat in a clearing in the woods, and because there was sunlight, there was grass. Connie examined the grass and found a slightly worn footpath that led away from the camp.

"Let's follow the path and see where it leads. It might be an animal path, but again it might be a human path," she suggested.

"You're in charge," I said. "You've found lost people before, haven't you?"

"Yes, I have. But of course they wanted to be found. Bryan doesn't."

"Maybe on some level he does want to be found." I closed my eyes and felt a chill run up my spine. Somewhere in the recesses of my mind a connection was being made. For a moment I saw it clearly, and then it was gone. "We should definitely follow this path!"

The day was becoming hot. The high pressure system that was heading eastward earlier in the week, must have arrived. We stopped for lunch, which thankfully Connie had brought along from the lodge's kitchen.

"Is it my imagination, or have we been walking up hill for the last half hour?" I asked.

"We have, indeed. Up ahead is an outcropping of rock. If Bryan is here, then that's the most likely place for him to be hiding."

"Is it far?" I asked. I had just about run out of steam for all this Great Outdoors crap!

"We've only walked a little over a mile, Jesse. But no, it's not far. We'll leave our backpacks here and walk as quietly as we can toward the rocks."

I stood up and brushed the pine needles off my jeans, re-tied my boot straps and was ready to go. We walked in single file with Connie leading. After about ten minutes I could see the outcropping of rocks up ahead. Like a small mountain, it showed above the tops of the trees.

171

Connie signaled me to stop and we listened. We heard some faint sounds that seemed to be coming from up ahead. We moved slowly and saw a movement in a clearing up ahead. I could smell the faint odor of smoke drifting through the trees. We walked ahead a few more feet and crouched behind a large rock to watch.

The young man, though looking somewhat unkempt, fit Bryan's description. He was busy stirring a pot that was suspended over small fire. From all appearances Bryan was alone.

"You can take it from here," whispered Connie.

I stood up and took several steps before Bryan saw me. A look of panic showed on his face and then he turned quickly around looking for an escape route.

"Bryan! I yelled. "I'm Jesse Ashworth. Your father sent me to find you!"

Bryan looked around and then collapsed on the ground with his head hidden in his hands, and began sobbing uncontrollably.

Chapter 25

The air was hot and dry as the warm front moved east across Maine, reaching the seacoast by early evening. The heat was expected to be with us for several days with ninety plus temperatures. By the end of the week a cold front was expected to arrive and bring thunder showers that would usher in cooler weather.

Bryan had dried his tears and reluctantly agreed to come back to Bath with me. As soon as I was able to pick up cell service, I called Tim to let him know that I had Bryan with me. Tim would let Bryan's father know that he was safe, but for Bryan's safety we would have to keep his return secret.

"You think he's really in danger?" asked Tim.

"Big time!" I answered. "I'll explain when we get home. For the time being I think Bryan needs to stay with us.

"Drive safely," said Tim.

"I always do!"

....

Connie Thurston dropped us off at the inn. I collected my things while Bryan went in to say good-bye to Martha Rankin. I wasn't sure if I should let him out of my sight or not, but he was ready to go when I went to the kitchen to collect him. Martha put up a bag of goodies for us to take. I was pretty sure Bryan was in need of some good food. The five hour drive back would be tiresome after a long day.

At first Bryan was very quiet, but I knew that by the end of the trip I'd have the complete story.

"I don't know where to begin," said Bryan after a few miles. That was a good sign as it meant that he trusted me.

"Let me help," I offered. "I put a few things together, but you can help me fill in the blanks. You were taking an art class with Kelley Kennedy."

"How did you know that?"

"I'm a detective." I had been waiting a long time to say that with a straight face to someone! "It was you who painted the forgery of *The Majorette* and Kelley posed for the painting."

"I didn't know until later that she was going to use it as a forgery. I thought I was painting a copy."

"It was her idea to use it as a forgery?" I didn't see that one coming.

"Not in the beginning, I don't think. I think that idea came later. At first we did it as an assignment. She posed for me and I painted her. When she saw how good my painting was, she arranged for us to paint in the museum and use the real painting as a model."

"When did you go to the museum? Usually they don't allow visitors in the gallery with a paint brush!"

"Kelley and I both worked at the museum. I worked in security and she was head of donor relations." That was true, they both were on staff. But I also knew from working there in security that their passes wouldn't allow her to come in after six.

"Someone else must have known that you two were in the museum. Who let you in?"

"The director let us in."

"Bill Baker?"

"Yes," answered Bryan. The pieces were all falling into place and a picture was emerging from the chaos that had been swirling around in my head.It wasn't a pretty picture either!

"Did you get the sense that he knew what she was up to?"

"Of course! They were having an affair!"

"They were?" Once again I'd been blindsided. "When did you figure out that they were up to something?"

"At first I thought Bill Baker was helping us with an assignment. When I learned that they were having an affair, I put two and two together, but the painting was almost finished."

"Why didn't you walk away then?" I asked. I was pretty sure I knew the answer, but I'd let Bryan confirm it for me.

"He said he'd kill me if I told anyone. He said that the painting was my work and he and Kelley would testify that I painted the forgery and that they knew nothing about it. They said I'd go to jail for a long time."

"So you finished the painting?"

"No, not quite. I left something out."

"How did you know?"

"I told you before, I'm a detective!"

....

Tim and Al Landry were waiting for us when we pulled up to Eagle's Nest later that evening. Bryan was exhausted emotionally. He hadn't known that Kelley was dead. The murder happened after he had run away. That news put more fear into him. We all decided that he should stay with Tim and me for a few days. We would take him to the police station in Portland

175

tomorrow. After the father-son reunion, we fed Bryan and sent him off to bed. I told Tim and Al all I had learned.

"I'm not sure I understand the whole thing," said Al.

"It's all been an elaborate plot of confusion. Bill Baker intended to replace *The Majorette* with a forgery and sell the original painting. Then he got greedy or he got scared that someone would figure out that the painting was a forgery. At any rate he planned to collect the insurance and skim some of the money off the top. He was as surprised as anyone when we found the forgery he had hidden in the air vent."

"How do you know all this?" asked Al.

"Mostly from listening to Bryan's story and filling in the blanks. I'm sure the police can figure out the rest."

"But if he was guilty why did he call us in to investigate?" asked Tim.

"He called us in for several reasons. The first reason was so that we would be the ones to find the bodies. How convenient that he happened to have a private security firm there at the time. The second reason is that we were a new company. He gambled on the fact that we were new and not too bright."

"He obviously was wrong," observed Al.

"What about the hauntings?" asked Tim.

"That was just a diversion. It kept us busy trying to prove that there were no ghosts. It also diverted the news away from the murders."

"So why did he kill Kelley Kennedy?" asked Al.

"Maybe he wanted all the money for himself. I'd like to think that she didn't realize his plan until much later."

"So he killed her to keep her quiet?" asked Al.

"I think so!" Al looked stricken. I knew he realized just how close Bryan had come to being a murder victim himself.

"And Janet Costa," said Tim, picking up on the thread of the story, "was an outside auditor. She must have found some discrepancies in the books. He killed her to keep his embezzlement from being discovered."

"I think the police will have a few questions to ask William Baker," I replied with a yawn. "But right now I'm exhausted and need my beauty sleep."

"I should get going. Jesse, I don't know how to thank you for finding my son. I'll head home and let you rest," Al Landry already looked ten years younger.

"Come back tomorrow for breakfast, and then we'll all go in to the police station," offered Tim.

177

Chapter 26

I t was late in the evening when the thunderstorms hit the Maine coast. The wind, thunder and lightning made a dramatic end to what had been a dramatic week. Several fires in town had been started by lightning strikes, but there had been little damage and no injuries. The hot heavy air had been replaced by a cooler and drier air mass that had dipped down from Canada.

Tim and I had taken Bryan Landry in to the Portland police, where he signed a statement. No charges would be brought against Bryan if he agreed to testify. It took several days for the police to complete their investigation, but the end result was that William Baker, director of the Turner Museum, was arrested for the theft of a major work of art, and for the murders of Kelley Kennedy and Janet Costa. As expected, William Baker claimed to be innocent of the murders, though he confessed to arranging the theft of the painting.

The Big Boys' Detective Agency had now cleared all its major cases, and we had solved them in a little less than two months. I was planning to take a few days off, now that we had no major cases to work on. Tim and Derek could handle the alarm business for a few days while I did some prep work for the upcoming Fourth of July Clam Bake and wedding.

Rhonda and Jackson were due home from their cruise and Argus and I were on our way to Camden to pick them up. The drive along Route One from Bath to Camden was slower than usual because of the summer tourist traffic. I had the windows and the sunroof open because of the cool fresh summer air and the occasional smell of the ocean. Argus was sitting in the front seat, harnessed in with a doggy seatbelt, but still able to get his nose close enough to the window to enjoy the smells as we slowly sailed down the road.

Because of the slow traffic, I managed to pull into Camden and find a parking spot near the library at the head of the harbor just as the *Doris Dean* was releasing its passengers. I waved to Rhonda and Jackson as they headed up the hill with their bags. I don't know where she got it, but Rhonda was dressed in a white sailor's outfit with a sailor's hat perched at a rakish angle on her head. To his credit, Jackson was dressed in jeans and a polo shirt, like a normal person.

"Hey, Jackson, good to see you! You, too, Pop Eye!" I greeted them.

"Don't be an asshole!" replied Rhonda.

"Good to see you, too," offered Jackson.

"How was the trip?" I asked.

"It was amazing," said Jackson as I threw their bags in the trunk. "We met up with about ten tall ships and about twenty other vessels as well. There was a full moon over the water and we had some musicians on board, so we had live music every night."

"And the food!" supplied Rhonda. "The food was incredible. Everything was homemade and made from scratch. One night we went ashore to a small island in Penobscot Bay and had a clam bake."

"So you both had a good time?"

"Oh, yes!" they answered in unison.

"Now it's back to real life, I guess," sighed Rhonda. We got in the car and began the ride back home.

"Summer hasn't really even started yet," I said as I eased the car out into the traffic of Route One. "Tim and I are having a backyard clam bake for the Fourth of

July with a little surprise, so plan on attending. Which reminds me, Jessica wants a fashion consultation. I think she actually likes your vintage stylings."

"I'd be happy to help. By the way, what's new with you?"

I told them about my trip to Beaver Lake and about finding Bryan Landry and the revelations about the crimes.

"Holy shit!" exclaimed Jackson. "You have been busy, haven't you. So Bill Baker killed Kelley Kennedy and the auditor?"

"Yes, it appears so." But as I said it I had a nagging feeling that I missed something. But I convinced myself that it was just my imagination and stress talking.

About an hour later we pulled into the driveway of their house. Tim and Viola were there to greet us. We all helped unload the bags. Tim had picked up some Italian sandwiches and chips for lunch.

We sat in the kitchen and chatted over lunch. After we finished lunch, Rhonda went off to unpack and Tim, Viola and I went out on the porch to finish our beers. Rhonda and Jackson had a great view of the river from their Victorian house, and the three of us fell silent as we watched two power boats speed up the river toward Augusta.

Suddenly the silence was interrupted by a blood-curdling scream coming from Rhonda's bedroom. Viola leaned over and whispered something to Jackson and then gave me a wink.

Rhonda rushed out to the porch. "I've been robbed!" she screamed. "My jewelry is gone!" None of us got up.

"I don't think so," I said as I took another sip of beer.

"Unlikely!" added Jackson.

"You're crazy!" chimed in Viola.

"My jewelry case is empty!" cried Rhonda.

"You mean you're missing these?" Viola reached into her handbag and pulled out a handful of jewelry.

"What…" stammered Rhonda.

"You crazy bimbo!" I said as I jumped up. "You asked us both to look after your house and gave us both keys, but you neglected to mention that little fact to either of us. We were both in the house, thinking that we had an intruder. I had my gun drawn and scared Viola to death!"

"You had to be punished!" added Viola.

"You see dear," said Jackson, "you are forgetful." He turned to us. "She claims I'm making it up when she forgets to tell me something."

"We're all forgetful," said Tim. "Start taking notes like the rest of us."

"Assholes!" muttered Rhonda as she took a seat on the porch with us.

....

The beautiful weather continued and the weather forecasters predicted that the Fourth of July would have great weather. Of course that was days away and anything could change between now and then, but it gave me hope for a good holiday.

I was sitting at my desk in the office when Jessica buzzed me on the intercom.

"Jim Freeman to see you, Jesse."

"Thanks, Jessica. Send him in. Tell Tim I'm in a meeting"

"Good morning, Jesse. I just came in to settle up my account and thank you for finding Kelley's killer. They're charging William Baker with two counts of homicide." Jim seemed to be much more relaxed than I'd ever seen him.

"Have a seat Jim." Something in my head flashed as the last piece of the murder puzzle fell into place.

"I didn't think you had much of a chance of finding Kelley's killer."

"I almost didn't."

"But William Baker is in jail, isn't he? You did good work."

"Yes, Baker did commit murder. The problem is that he only committed one murder."

"What do you mean?"

"We've all been assuming that the same person committed both murders. The one thing we all seemed to overlook is that Kelley was dressed up in a costume when she was killed. That part just doesn't fit. Dressing someone up before they are murdered is more a crime of passion, not one of greed. Whoever killed Kelley did so out of emotional anger, not greed or fear."

"Then who killed her?" Jim asked.

"You did!"

"You're crazy!" Jim's expression changed.

"You found out about the affair and Kelley must have told you what she and Baker were up to. You probably killed her by accident. There was a wound on the back of her head. She must have fallen and hit her head when you two struggled. Once she was dead, you panicked. Then you thought of a fitting way to get back

182

at Baker. You dressed her up like *The Majorette* and placed her on the loading dock of the museum. It was a message to Baker, but you didn't count on us being there and finding the body. Once you found out that I was not just a private security guard, but was also one of Kelley's ex-husbands, you had to find a way to get me off the trail. You decided to convince Jeff Hastings to hire me to help clear your name, and then when you got out of jail you hired me under the pretext of finding the real killer. How am I doing so far?"

Jim Freeman looked at me with a mixture of fear and hate. In the half opened door to the office, I caught a glimpse of Tim standing off to one side signaling to someone.

Then you staged a break-in of your own house. Conveniently Kelley's clothes were gone and her computer was stolen. You wanted it to look like you were the victim. And the icing on the cake was when you broke into my house and stole my laptop, thinking I might keep my case notes on my home computer. Anything I'm leaving out or is that pretty much what happened?"

Jim shook his head. He grabbed a paperweight off my desk as if he planned to bean me on the head with it. But then he crumpled and dropped the paperweight on the floor and placed his head in his hands."

"Is that a yes?" I asked.

He nodded his head.

"James Freeman, you better come with me," said Officer Derek Cooper as he stepped into the room. Tim had gotten my message about "being in a meeting." That was a code word for "pay attention!" Tim had sent for Derek and he and Derek had been standing in the doorway listening to the last part of the exchange.

Derek looked every bit the cop in charge as he led Jim Freeman away.

"Are you okay?" asked Tim with a real look of concern.

"I'm so stupid," I said shaking my head, "I should have seen it earlier. I should have put two and two together."

"The miracle," said Tim taking my hand, "is that you figured it out at all. No one else, including the police, was able to do that."

Chapter 27

It was a very peaceful and a very sad place. It was a place that made people avert their eyes as they passed by on the road. It was the last stop for many on their journey through life. Oak Grove Cemetery, like many nineteenth century graveyards, was a garden cemetery. There were weeping willow trees, evergreens, and reflecting ponds. Yet despite the attempt at landscaping, there really was only one purpose to the place.

I had come to pay my final respects at Kelley's grave. The last two months had seemed surreal, but now with the conclusion of the case, I allowed myself time to reflect on life and death. I didn't know what Kelley had become, but I did know who she used to be. Back in college she was a red-headed, nineteen year-old spitfire. We had a blast all through college and beyond, and then we moved in different directions. But I knew that part of her would always be that girl I knew.

I felt the tears well up in my eyes and spill down my cheeks. Suddenly I was enfolded by a set of strong arms, arms that held me until I was ready to face the rest of the day.

"How did you know I was here?" I asked as I turned to face Tim.

"Because I know you, and I knew you would be here."

"And you followed me when I left the house."

"There is that."

"Thank you. I thought I wanted to be alone, but I am very glad you are here." Tim reached up and wiped the tears from my eyes.

"Now come away, we have a busy day of celebrations. And later the two of us are going to sit on the back porch of Eagle's Nest and watch the fireworks over the river.

....

By all accounts the Fourth of July Parade through downtown Bath was great. Tim and I, however, were too busy setting up for the clam bake, birthday party, and wedding! The florist had dropped off buckets of daisies. The rental company had dropped off the folding chairs and Billy and Jason were setting up for the clambake.

Jessica and Derek, as seems the case with most young people, were taking it all in stride. Tim, however, was a nervous wreck, and I was running around the backyard making sure all the details were in place.

This was supposed to be an informal gathering of friends and family, but our guest list had grown to over twenty, which I guess, compared to most weddings, was small enough. The wedding cake arrived and I was grateful that Jessica hadn't insisted on my making it.

Finally I had all the chairs arranged by the gazebo, the musicians had arrived, and the first of the guests had begun showing up. I watched in fascination as the clambake was laid out. First they had lined the fire pit with rocks and built a roaring fire, later in the morning they had raked away the coals and lined the pit with seaweed, then they put in the Portuguese sausage, the clams, mussels, and lobsters, layered on more seaweed, and then covered it all with a wet tarp. I knew when it was done that we would have a perfectly cooked meal.

A Sagadahoc Nursing Home Van arrived carrying Beatrice Lafond. It was her one hundredth birthday, and all of us who grew up in Bath had her as our English teacher.

"Jesse," Mrs. Lafond said as I helped her into a special chair. "I hope you live long enough to have a birthday like this of your own!"

"Thanks, Mrs. Lafond."

"Where's Timmy?"

"Timmy," I replied, "Is most likely having a nervous breakdown."

"Thanks for springing me out of that nursing home. Now go and find Tim."

Tim and Derek were in the kitchen drinking what I hoped was coffee.

"Time for us to get dressed," I said. "Where's Jessica?"

"She's in the bedroom dressing. Rhonda is helping her," replied a grim looking Tim.

It was time to start the ceremony. Jessica had picked out our clothes. Nothing traditional here! Tim and I were wearing matching gray slacks, white shirt with yellow ties, and gray 1940's hats. Derek was dressed like us, except that he had on a yellow shirt and a white tie. Actually we made a striking trio. I just hoped in years to come, Jessica wouldn't look at the wedding photos and shudder.

The yellow and white was decked out with yellow and white daisies. Derek and I made our way to the gazebo as the crowd gathered in their seats. Jessica had chosen a cellist and a flutist as the music and they began playing a soft classical tune. Everyone looked to the rear as Jessica and Tim approached. And then there was silence.

Jessica was dressed in a long white dress with yellow trim. She had daisies in her hair and made one of the most beautiful brides I had ever seen. She was an ethereal beauty, like the subject of a Pre-Raphaelite painting. I looked at Derek and he was staring at her like it was the first time he had seen her!

Everyone stood up as Jessica and Tim walked down the aisle. The Reverend Mary Bailey climbed the up the gazebo steps and faced the crowd.

"Behold the power of love! Today is a celebration! The days to come may be challenging or joy-filled. We have no power over tomorrow. But today we have a choice. Today we can be happy. This is a celebration of three events. Today we celebrate the birth of our country. Let us always remember those who sacrificed for us so that we may rejoice today! It is also the one hundredth birthday of a beloved and respected teacher whom many of you had! Happy birthday Beatrice!" And of course it is Jessica and Derek's wedding day. Look around at your friends and see what love has gathered together. This is the power of love!

The wedding was beautiful, the clambake was delicious, and the yard had been cleaned up and everything put away. The sun had set, and Tim and I were sitting on the back porch waiting for the fireworks. Argus had curled up in a ball and was sleeping on the seat between us.

"This was a good day," said Tim as the first of the fireworks lit up the night sky."

"It certainly was. Everything turned out perfectly." We sat for a time watching the fireworks. Argus didn't seem the least bit annoyed by the booming sounds. I felt Tim take my hand in the dark.

"Do you believe in the power of love?" he asked.

"Yes, Tim. I do!"

Recipes from Jesse Ashworth's Kitchen

Honey and Molasses Cake

This is a recipe from WWII when sugar was rationed.

1 ¼ cup of flour   ¼ tsp cinnamon
1 tsp baking soda   ¼ tsp cloves
¼ tsp salt   ¼ tsp allspice
¼ tsp nutmeg   ¼ cup honey
1 egg   ½ molasses
¼ cup oil   ½ cup boiling water

Preheat oven to 350. Mix all ingredients together, adding boiling water last. Bake in a tube pan for 35 minutes.

Lobster Stew
Fresh lobster makes the best stew. Save the juice when you crack open the shells and add to the stew.

2 cups cooked lobster meat   1 small onion
½ stick butter   2 cups light cream
2 cups of milk
Melt butter in large saucepan with onion. Add lobster meat and juice and cook for three minutes. Add milk and cream and refrigerate.

Molasses Pie
This is the Maine recipe similar to the southern version of Shoo fly pie.
Preheat oven to 400 Thaw one frozen pie crust, or make one pie crust from scratch.

Combine in Bowl:
      1 cup of flour
      5 tbsp butter
      2/3 cup of brown sugar
      Mash until crumbly

In a separate bowl:
      1 cup of molasses
      1 egg
      1 tsp baking soda
      1 cup boiling water

Take half of the crumb mixture and molasses mix and pour into piecrust. Top with the remaining crumb mixture. Bake for 10 minutes and reduce heat to 350 for 20-30 minutes. Serve with whipped cream

191

Egg Bread (for bread machine)
This make a 1 ½ lb loaf

2 eggs	1 cup warm water
2 tbsp oil	2 tbsp sugar
1 ½ tsp salt	2 cups white flour
1 cup whole wheat flour	
1 ½ tsp yeast.	

Use basic setting on machine.

Blueberry Cream Cheese Pie
This is a great way to enjoy fresh Maine blueberries.

1 baked pie shell	1 tbsp lemon juice
4 cups of fresh blueberries	
1 (6oz) package of cream cheese	
¾ cup water	½ powdered sugar
¼ cup of tapioca	whipped cream

Simmer 2 cups of blueberries in water for 4 minutes. Add combined sugar and tapioca to the cooking fruit. Continue until syrup is thick. Add lemon juice and remove from heat. Stir in remaining fresh blueberries. Set aside to cool.

Combine powdered sugar and cream cheese. Spread the cream cheese mixture in the bottom of the pie crust. Pour in blueberry mixture and chill. Serve with whipped cream.

Ambrosia Fruit Salad
A cool fruit salad treat on a hot day.

1 can (11oz) can mandarin oranges -drained
1 can (20 oz) pineapple chunks –drained
1/3 cup shredded coconut
½ cup miniature marshmallows
½ plain yogurt
Mix together and chill. Add mint leaves or maraschino cherries to garnish

Fruit upside down cake.
Looks great, but very easy to make.

Preheat oven to 350. Grease a round, deep cake pan. Use apple, pear, peaches, or pineapple.
Cake:

2/3 cup sugar	1 1/2 tsp baking powder
2/3 cup milk	½ stick unsalted butter
1 tbsp vanilla	

Topping: Fruit

2 tbsp butter	1/3 cup brown sugar	1tbsp water

Melt sugar and butter in microwave until syrup is formed. Spread bottom of pan with syrup. Place sliced fruit in bottom of pan. Cover with cake batter. Bake at 350 for 30 minutes or until done. Cool and turn out cake onto plate.

Orange cake
This cake has a subtle flavor and light texture.

½ cup of oil   ¾ cup of sugar
zest from one orange
2 large eggs   ½ cup sour cream
¼ cup orange juice   1 ½ cup flour
1 tsp baking powder   ½ tsp baking soda
½ tsp salt

Mix together and bake in a tube pan 350 degrees for 30 minutes.

Biscuits (Food Processor)
Preheat oven to 400
1 ¾ cup flour   ½ tsp salt
3 tsp baking powder   ½ tsp soda
6 tbsp cold butter   2 tbsp shortening
Place dry mixture in food processor and pulse until coarsely mixed.
Add ¾ milk and pulse until combined. Roll out, cut biscuits and bake on ungreased pan at 400 for 12 minutes.

Squash Soup

2 large squashes cup up and microwaved.
2 cup chicken or vegetable broth
2 tbsp butter   1 package cream cheese.
4 tbsp honey   1 tbsp salt
¼ tsp nutmeg   ¼ tsp ginger
¼ cup milk.
Heat slowly and put in blender, or use an emersion
blender to create a smooth soup.

Vegetarian Slow Cooker Chile

½ cup olive oil   2 tsp salt
4 onions chopped   ½ tsp black pepper
1 green pepper sliced   1 red pepper sliced
6 tbsp chili powder   2 tsp cumin
2 tbsp oregano   1 (14 oz) Package of firm tofu,
drained and finely cubed
2 cans drained black beans
2 cans drained red beans
2 tbsp vinegar   1 tbsp hot sauce
2 cans crushed tomatoes
¼ cup ground carrots
Brown peppers and onion with the tofu in oil until
slightly browned. Pour all ingredients in slow cooker
and cook on low for 6 to 8 hours.

195

Bean Salad
1 can each drained kidney beans, chick peas, white beans, black beans
1 small can of corn
½ lb of cooked green beans
1 package frozen lima beans cooked
1 chopped onion
1/3 cup sugar
1/3 cup vinegar
1 tsp dry mustard
¼ cup oil.

Combine all ingredients and chill.

Roast Potatoes

Cut up potatoes and place in a plastic bag.
Add one chopped onion, salt and pepper
¼ cup bread crumbs to the bag.
Add 2 tbsp olive oil and shake bag.
Bake at 350 until done.

New Potatoes and Peas
Peel and cook new potatoes in boiling water. Add 1 package frozen peas and cook until peas are ready. Drain, add ½ cup of heavy cream and 2 tbsp butter, Salt and pepper and serve,

Minted Peas

Cook frozen peas in water. Drain, add butter and ¼ cup crème de menthe. Serve.

Red Cabbage

Cut red cabbage into wedges and steam for about 30 minutes. Toss cabbage with butter and olive oil. Add 2 tbsp of horse radish and serve.

Oven Beef Stew

2 tbsp flour	2 tsp salt
Pepper to taste	2 cups water
1 lb stew beef	1 cup tomato soup
1 chopped onion	3 potatoes
2 chopped carrots	2 tbsp

Combine salt , pepper and flour and dredge meat. Brown meat in butter. Place in oven proof dish the meat, soup , onion, and 1 cup of water at 375 for one hour. Add vegetables and the rest of the water and cook for another hour.

Slow Cooker Chicken Cordon Bleu

Boneless chicken breasts; one per person.
¼ lb sliced cheese
¼ lb sliced ham
1 can condensed cream of chicken or cream of
mushroom soup

*Place breasts in plastic wrap and pound flat. Layer thin
ham slices and thin slices of cheese on top of breasts.
Roll each breast and secure with a tooth pick.
Place in oiled slow cooker . Cover with soup. Cool on
low.*

Beef Casserole

1 lb lean chuck cut into 1 inch cubes.
½ cup red wine
1 can beef consommé
Salt and pepper
1 chopped onion
¼ cup bread crumbs
¼ cup flour
¼ cup ground carrots
Mix and cover, bake in a 350 oven for 3 hours.

Spaghetti Pie

1 8 oz package of spaghetti (broken into little pieces.)
2 tbsp olive oil
1 jar of spaghetti sauce
1/3 cup grated parmesan cheese
1 egg
1 ½ lb ground beef (or half beef and half ground Italian sausage)
1 onion
½ tsp oregano
1 cup cottage or ricotta cheese
1 package mixed shredded cheese.
¼ cup red wine

Cook spaghetti, drain and place in bowl. Add egg and parmesan cheese. Spread mixture evenly in 9" x 13" pan. Brown meat and onion, stir in spaghetti sauce, red wine, sugar, and oregano with the meat.

Spread cottage or ricotta cheese. Sprinkle half of the shredded cheese over cheese mixture. Cover with meat mixture. Sprinkle remaining shredded cheese and bake at 350 for 30 minutes.

Cheeseburger Pie

1 lb. ground beef	1 chopped onion
½ tsp. salt	½ tsp. pepper
1 cup cheddar cheese	1 ½ cup. milk
2 cups biscuit mix	
3 eggs	

Brown meat with onions and peppers. Drain. Mix biscuit mixture, salt, pepper, eggs and milk. Grease bottom and sides of 9 x 13-inch pan. Spread meat in pan. Sprinkle cheese over meat. Pour batter over cheese. Bake at 350 degrees for 1 hour.

Slow Cooker Lasagna

1 lb ground beef or Italian sausage
1 chopped onion
1 (28 oz) can tomato sauce
1 (6oz) can tomato paste
1 ½ tsp salt
1 tsp dried Italian seasoning
12 oz cottage cheese
¼ cup grated parmesan or Romano cheese
½ cup shredded cheddar cheese 12 (oz) uncooked lasagna noodles

Brown beef and onion in fry pan, drain excess grease. Add tomato sauce and tomato paste, salt and spices. Spoon some meat sauce of the bottom of the slow cooker. Add a layer of uncooked noodles (break to fit the pot is needed.) Top with cheese mixture. Add another layer of meat sauce. Layer more noodles, cheese and meat sauce until used up. Cook on low for about five hours.